INDIAN PRAIRIE PUBLIC LIBRARY DISTRICT

3 1946 00598 9816

O9-BTL-762

N nut

O owl

P present

Q queen

R rug

S spider

T turtle

U umbrella

V vase

W walrus

X xiphias

xylophone

Y yarn

Z zipper

A GOLDEN BOOK • NEW YORK

Richard Scarry's Best Word Book Ever copyright © 1963, renewed 1991 by Random House, Inc.,
copyright © 1980 by Richard Scarry.
Richard Scarry's Cars and Trucks and Things That Go copyright © 1974, renewed 2002 by Richard Scarry II.
Richard Scarry's Busy, Busy Town copyright © 1994 by the Estate of Richard Scarry.
All rights reserved. Published in the United States by Golden Books, an imprint of Random House Children's Books,
a division of Random House, Inc., 1745 Broadway, New York, NY 10019, and in Canada by Random House of Canada
Limited, Toronto. This collection was originally published in the United States as *Richard Scarry's Biggest and Best
Storybook Ever* by Golden Books Publishing Company, Inc., New York, in 1998, and is comprised of three works originally
published in 1963 and revised in 1974, 1980, and 1994. Golden Books, A Golden Book, the G colophon, and the distinctive
gold spine are registered trademarks of Random House, Inc.
www.randomhouse.com/kids
Library of Congress Control Number: 2009927206
ISBN: 978-0-375-85483-5
Printed in the United States of America
10 9 8 7 6 5

Richard Scarry's
Biggest, Busiest Storybook Ever

Featuring

BUSY, BUSY TOWN

CARS and TRUCKS and THINGS THAT GO

BEST WORD BOOK EVER

INDIAN PRAIRIE PUBLIC LIBRARY
401 Plainfield Rd.
Darien, IL 60561

Contents

Richard Scarry's BUSY,

BUSY TOWN

It's a fine morning in Busytown.
Everyone is rushing to work.
Let's see where they're going.

Office Workers

Many people work in offices, like this lawyer. If two people have an argument, lawyers try to settle it.

There are all kinds of writers. The best writers write children's books.

PUBLIC LIBRARY

Librarians lend people books from the library. The best librarians are children's book librarians.

Artists paint pictures. The best artists paint pictures for children's books.

The best window washers do not drop their pails of water!

BANK

This is a bank. We keep our money here, where it will be safe.

A guard stands by the door of the bank.

Messengers quickly deliver packages to offices all over town.

On Main Street

There are all kinds of shops and stores on Busytown's Main Street.

You can wash your clothes.
Oh, dear! The washing machine
is leaking.

Water is coming out of
the laundromat.

You can get your shoes fixed.

You can buy candy and books.

On Main Street you can buy medicine, tools, apples, and oranges. You can even get a haircut.

At the Post Office

Huckle writes a
letter to Grandma.

He takes it to the post office, where a postal
worker weighs the letter. Then the postal worker
puts a stamp on the letter. Another postal worker
uses a rubber stamp to cancel the letter. Now the
letter shows the date it was mailed.

A sorter puts all the letters going
to Grandma's town in one bag. All
the other letters go in other bags.

The mail truck driver takes
the mailbags to the airport.

The mailbags are loaded onto airplanes. The bag with the letter to Grandma is flown to the post office in Grandma's town.

There is a letter carrier for each neighborhood in Grandma's town.

Grandma's letter carrier puts Huckle's letter into his bag.

GRANDMA CAT

Grandma is happy to receive a letter from Huckle, isn't she?

The Busytown School

The bus driver is taking these children to school.

Miss Honey is the schoolteacher. She reads stories to her students . . .

1 2 3 4 5 6 7 8 9 10

and helps them learn to count to ten.

A B C D E F G H I J K L M N O P Q R S T U V W X Y Z

Miss Honey asks Lowly to write the alphabet
on the chalkboard. Good work, Lowly!

Janitor Joe keeps the schoolhouse neat and clean.
He has come to wash the windows in the classroom.
Oh, dear! The pupils may be washed instead.
"Class dismissed," says Miss Honey.

17

Busy Housekeepers

Everyone helps out around the house.
Busy workers make a happy home.

A cook

A dish washer

A table setter

A wastebasket emptier

A floor sweeper

A clothes picker-up

A vacuumer

A bed maker

18

A tricycle painter

A fallen-leaf carrier

A window washer

A garden hoer

A garden waterer

A grass raker

A dirt mover

A lawn mower

A strawberry gatherer

19

Lowly Goes to the Medical Center

It's time for Lowly to have a checkup. The nurse at the medical center greets him. "Hello, Lowly," she says. "Dr. Lion will see you now."

"Your weight is just about right for such a skinny fellow," says Dr. Lion.

Dr. Dentist looks into Lowly's mouth. "Very good, Lowly," she says. "You have no cavities."

Now Lowly gets his eyes checked. "Lowly, tell me what you see on the eye chart," says the eye doctor. "Apples," says Lowly.

"You have very good eyes, Lowly," says Dr. Rabbit.

Dr. Lion checks Lowly's throat. "Open your mouth and say, 'Aaah,'" says Dr. Lion. "Very good!"

Nurse Nelly takes Lowly to
visit a patient with a broken leg.
Poor patient!
Nurses are good at taking care of people.

Lowly has an X ray taken.
"Your insides look good,
Lowly," says the X ray taker.

This is an ambulance. The ambulance driver
brings patients to the medical center when
they have to be taken care of in a hurry.

Keeping Busytown Clean

Pig Will is in charge of the Pig family's garbage. He takes the garbage from the kitchen and puts it outside in the garbage can.

Joe Pig collects bottles and cans from all around town. He takes them to the recycling center.

PAPER

ALUMINUM   GLASS

Jim the junkman collects old furniture in his junk truck.

Susy Cat slept too late this morning. Get out of bed, Susy!

REFUSE HAULED AWAY

Tincan Cat, the town sanitation worker, empties his garbage truck at the garbage dump.

Squish Cat squashes the garbage down with his squasher-downer.

Miss Kittycat uses her bulldozer to cover the garbage with dirt.

Grass and trees are planted. Someday the garbage dump will be a lovely picnic ground.

Brave Fire Fighters

Fire fighters must be ready for a fire at any time. Sometimes the fire alarm bell rings when they are sleeping. Wake up, fellows! Slide down the pole and hurry to the fire!

The fire fighters hop into their fire engines.

The fire fighters attach
a hose from the pumper
truck to the fire hydrant.

A ladder truck

A pumper truck

They climb the ladders and put
out the fire with water from their hoses.
What brave fire fighters they are!

Fixer-upers

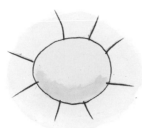

Mother Cat is having a bad day. Nothing seems to be working right. She has called many repair workers to fix things.

This man is replacing a broken window pane.

A TV repairman is fixing the television set.

A plumber is fixing the shower.

A locksmith is fixing a lock.

A telephone worker is fixing the telephone.

An appliance repairman is fixing the stove.

A roofer is fixing
a hole in the roof.

A chimney sweep is
cleaning the chimney.

This man is plastering
the wall.

A painter is painting
the walls.

A paperhanger is
papering the walls.

An electrician is putting
in new electric wires.

A furnace repairman
is fixing the furnace.

A plumber is fixing a leaky
water pipe. Hurry up, Mr. Plumber!

Lumber Workers

Many things are made of wood
We get our wood from trees.

Sometimes they cut a
tree down with a chain saw.

After they cut off the
branches, lumbermen cut
the tree trunk into logs.

Lumbermen cut down
big trees with their axes.

The logs are then pulled away to the sawmill
or put in a river to float downstream to a sawmill.

Workers at the sawmill use
giant saws to cut the logs into boards.

Carpenters use the boards to build
houses and many other things. Oh, dear.
This carpenter is not very lucky today.

Woodworkers

Here are many busy woodworkers making things with wood.

This worker is smoothing the top of a table with a sanding machine.

This worker is gluing the legs of a chair to the seat of a chair.

Helen is putting a wheel on the wagon she made.

Henry is taking a ride on the rocking horse he made.

George makes very fine beds to sleep in. He also makes chests to put clothes in.

Who is the busy box maker, I wonder?

A boat builder has built a fine rowboat and oars.
He is now going to row across the lake.

Barbie makes all kinds of toys with her jigsaw.

Wooden barrels can
hold all kinds of things.

Carpenters build wooden houses and barns.
Sometimes they hit their thumbs instead of
the nails with their hammers. OUCH!

This woodworker has just
made a toy sailboat.
What would you like to make?

Down on the Farm

Farmers work hard to feed us.
Farmer Haystack feeds corn to his
chickens so they will lay eggs for us to eat.

Mrs. Haystack gathers
eggs from the chickens' nests.

Farmer Pig feeds hay to his cow.
Cows give us milk to drink. MOOOO!

MILK

MILK

Farmer Fox plows his field.

Then he plants
wheat seeds in the field.

When the wheat grows tall, he
harvests the grain with his combine.

He takes the grain to the miller,
who grinds it into flour.

Able Baker Charlie buys flour
from the miller. He uses the
flour to make our bread. YUM!

FLOUR
XXXX

The Streets of Busytown

Lots of people work hard to keep our neighborhoods clean. This worker is washing the street clean with his special machine.

Some workers sweep up litter with their brooms.

Other workers sweep the street with their street sweepers.

A hot dog man sells hot dogs.

Some workers fix water pipes and electric wires which are buried under the street.

A worker digs into the pavement with his noisy jackhammer. He is going to fix a leaking water pipe.

A truck driver carries asphalt.

This worker is using the asphalt to fill up a pothole.

The newslady sells magazines and newspapers.

Hooray for the ice-cream man!

Cars and Trucks

There are many, many kinds of cars and trucks.
Lots of people use cars and trucks in their jobs.

The gardener uses his pickup
truck to haul plants and flowers.
He takes them to florists all
around Busytown.

Street lamp cleaners
sometimes drop things.
Be careful!

GARDENER

What does Pickles Pig
deliver in his pickle car?
Why, pickles, of course.

PICKLES

Trailer trucks haul things to stores all over town.
This truck is delivering fresh fruits and vegetables.

The cement mixer mixes cement
on the way to where a new building
is being built.

This is an armored car. It is used to
carry money from a bank. Robbers would
not be able to break into an armored car.

Lowly is a good
driver, isn't he?

Have you ever
seen a cheese car
on the highway?

At the Service Station

Garage workers take good care of our cars.

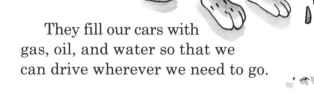

They fill our cars with gas, oil, and water so that we can drive wherever we need to go.

When something is wrong with the motor, the mechanic fixes it.

A garage worker uses a grease gun to help all the parts under the car run smoothly.

Sometimes a car breaks down on the road. The tow truck driver brings it to the garage to be fixed.

This worker is fixing a flat tire . . .

. . . and this one is washing a windshield.

Garage workers can make any car almost like new. Well—almost any car!

39

Railroad Workers

tank car

caboose

Rail yards are busy places.
Some railroad workers ride in a caboose.
The caboose is the last car on a train.

stationmaster

coal-powered
locomotive

oiler

conductor

signal

A worker fixes
a broken signal.

A hobo doesn't work, but
he likes to ride in a boxcar.

hobo

engineer

The freight train engineer watches the
signals. The signals tell him if he should
stop the train or keep on going.

The tower controller
sees that all the trains
stay on their own tracks.

control tower

cook

waiter

COACH

DINING
CAR

wheel inspector

A conductor collects the passengers'
tickets. The passengers are on their way to
the seashore. It is a long trip, but there is
plenty to eat in the dining car.

Would you like to ride on a train?

41

Around the Harbor

There is lots of work to do around a busy harbor. Would you like to work on a boat? A tugboat is small, but it can pull or push very heavy things.

tugboat captain

Oh, dear. The barge is on fire. But the fire fighters are putting it out right away.

fire fighters

buoy

fireboat

fisherman

forklift operator

This fisherman made a big catch today.

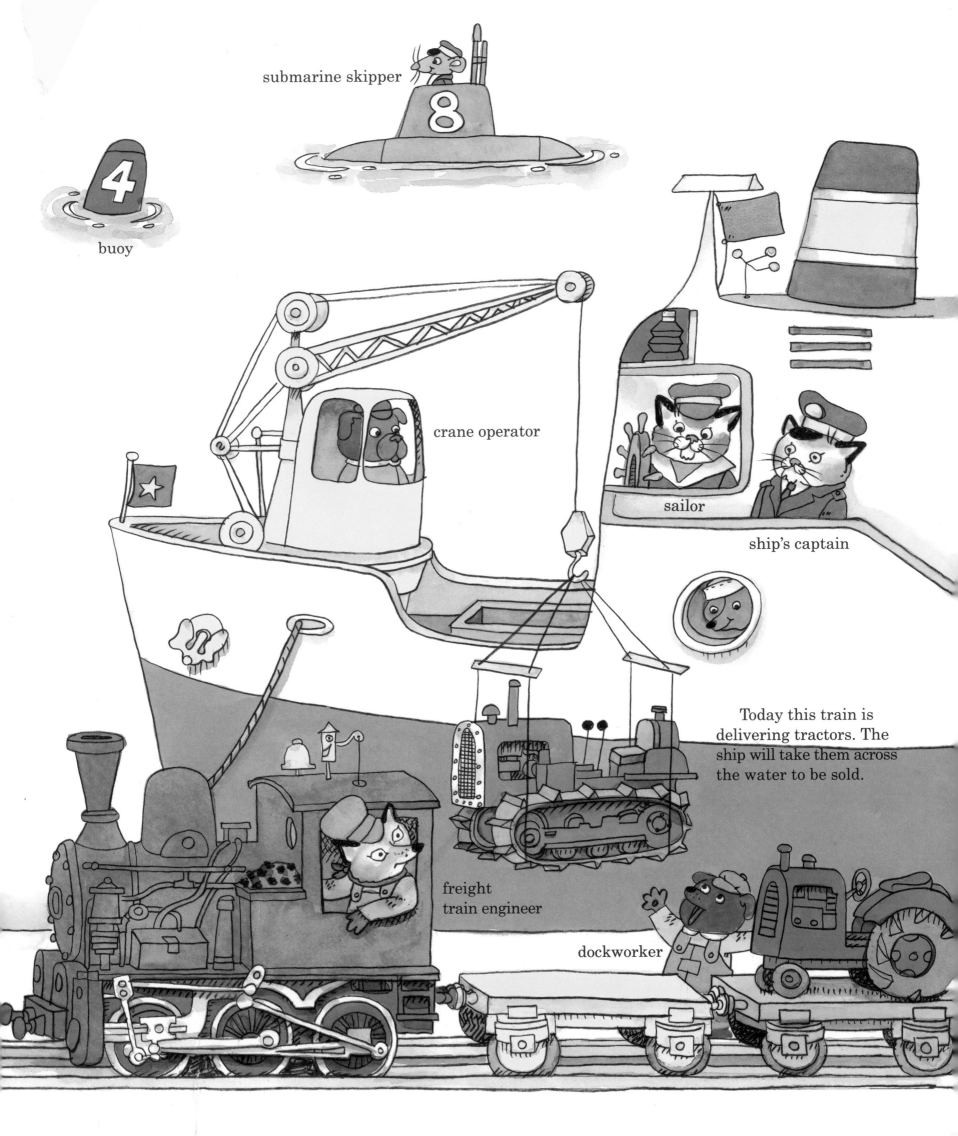

submarine skipper

buoy

crane operator

sailor

ship's captain

Today this train is delivering tractors. The ship will take them across the water to be sold.

freight train engineer

dockworker

At the Busytown Airport

An airport is a busy place. Many workers are
needed to help the airplanes take off and land safely.

A jet pilot zooms by
the jet control tower.

Air traffic controllers tell airplane pilots
when they can take off and when they can
land their planes.

A baggage handler takes baggage to a
waiting airplane.

A check-in clerk welcomes passengers.

A taxi driver drives a passenger to the airport.

A helicopter pilot can fly straight up or straight down. He can even stay still in the air.

The pilot of this jet plane is giving Lowly a special ride.

The flight attendant takes good care of all the passengers.

A businesswoman is boarding the airplane.

This man is filling the fuel tanks.

FUEL

This man directs planes at the terminal.

Oh, dear! A businessman is losing his important papers.

45

At the Supermarket

Do you like to go to the supermarket? People work there every day so that we will have good things to eat.

The baker makes cakes, cookies, and bread.

The butcher cuts up meat and grinds hamburger.

This stock clerk is bringing out fruits and vegetables.

A food delivery has just come in by truck. Every day more trucks come to the supermarket.

The dairy case keeps butter, milk, and yogurt cold.

This stock clerk has many cans of food to put on the shelves.

Shoppers pay the checkout clerk for the food they are buying.

47

Keeping Order in Busytown

Police officers do many different things during a busy day.

This police officer is telling these drivers when to stop and when to go.

Police officers take good care of lost children until their mothers come to get them.

Sometimes people park their cars where they are not supposed to. Police officers put parking tickets on those cars. The owners must then pay money to the town. That is called a fine.

Sergeant Murphy uses his motorcycle to chase speeding cars. Owners of speeding cars also have to pay money to the town, because speeding is very dangerous.

When there is an accident, it is a good thing to have a police officer around so that he can stop any quarrels.

Sergeant Murphy is going home to have dinner with his family. It is the end of a busy, busy day—in a busy, busy town. Good night, Sergeant Murphy!

49

Richard Scarry's
CARS and TRUCKS and THINGS THAT GO

THE 3 MOVERS

TENDER, LOVING, AND CARE

moving van

fuel oil truck

SANITATION ENGINEERS

garbage truck

garbage pails

auto-plane

FUEL

Have a nice trip!

garage

MISTRESS MOUSE REPAIRS

tow truck

mail van

Ma and Pa and Pickles and
Penny Pig are going on a picnic.
Here comes Ma with the
picnic basket.
Please hurry up, Ma.

MAIL

mailbox

51

SADIE'S
SODA FOUNTAIN
ALL FLAVORS

TOYS

SODY-POP

soft-drink truck

The Pigs are going to the beach to have their picnic.
But first, Pa has some shopping to do. He is going to order
some things to be delivered to their home.
I wonder what those things could be?

station wagon

SAM'S
SHOE
SHOP

shoe delivery car

old-time roadster

meter maid

52

drugstore delivery car

taxi

shopping cart

ABC GLASS COMPANY

bookstore delivery van

glass-window truck

old-time buggy

motorbikes

baby buggy

STOP

Did you see that? Dingo Dog has knocked down almost all the parking meters. What a terrible driver! I think Officer Flossy is going to give him a ticket. At least, she is going to try. We'll see if she succeeds.

Officer Flossy and her bicycle

a frightened parking meter

a terrible driver

hay wagon

sailboat

statue

delivery truck

HAY

MICHAEL ANGELO SCULPTOR

STOP

SOAPY SUDS WINDOW CLEANER

window washer

54

pickle truck

old-time roadster

Dingo drives off before Officer Flossy
can give him a ticket.
Oh, that Dingo is so naughty!
Go get him, Officer Flossy.

milk van

dragster

Pa Pig drives past a truck carrying a statue.
"Did you see who is in the back with the statue?"
Penny asks Pickles.
"Yes," says Pickles. "It's Goldbug. He shows up just
about everywhere."

alligator car

steam locomotive

caboose

trailer

MOLASSES

tank truck

tilt-cab truck

56

Where is Goldbug now?
Is he riding in the locomotive?
Is he riding in the old-time buggy?
Can you find him?

old-time buggy

go-cart

tractor

three-wheel beet truck

dumper

canvas-cab truck

unicycle

sports car

MISTRESS MOUSE REPAIRS

The Pig family drives by a broken-down truck.
"It won't be broken down for long," says Pa. "I saw
Mistress Mouse working on it. She can fix almost anything."

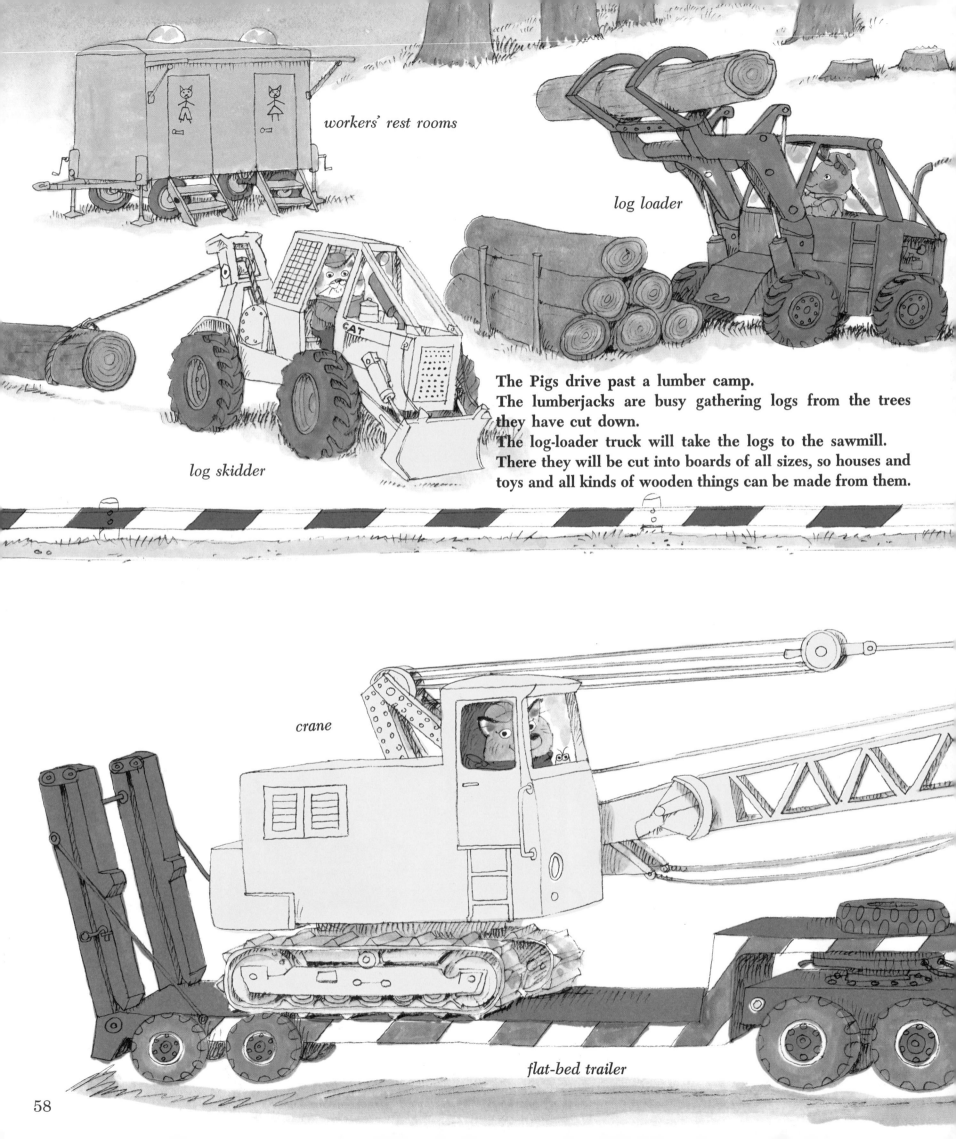

workers' rest rooms

log loader

log skidder

The Pigs drive past a lumber camp.
The lumberjacks are busy gathering logs from the trees they have cut down.
The log-loader truck will take the logs to the sawmill.
There they will be cut into boards of all sizes, so houses and toys and all kinds of wooden things can be made from them.

crane

flat-bed trailer

forklift truck

log-loader truck

"Oh, Bunny Rabbit, look out," calls Penny Pig. "Don't get caught by that crane!"

Step on the gas, Bunny Rabbit!

Faster, Flossy, faster!
Go get Dingo!
But where is that rascal?
Can you see him?

JAKE THE PLUMBER

double cab pick-up

mouse van

pumpkin car

tractor

mobile crane

Homer drove his tractor into the pond.
That wasn't very smart, Homer.

bus

woody station wagon

Look! There is Mistress Mouse again. And this time
she is towing a TOW TRUCK!
Hi there, Goldbug . . . wherever you are!

pig van

MISTRESS MOUSE REPAIRS

a wrecked car being towed
by a BIG TOW TRUCK which is being towed by a little tow truck

tourist bus

The baggage compartment on the bus has come open.
Someone's things are flying out!
Duck, Pa! Duck, Ma!
Oh dear, Ma didn't duck soon enough.

old-time fire engine

school mini-bus

dragster

MOTHER GOOSE
NURSERY SCHOOL

cheese truck

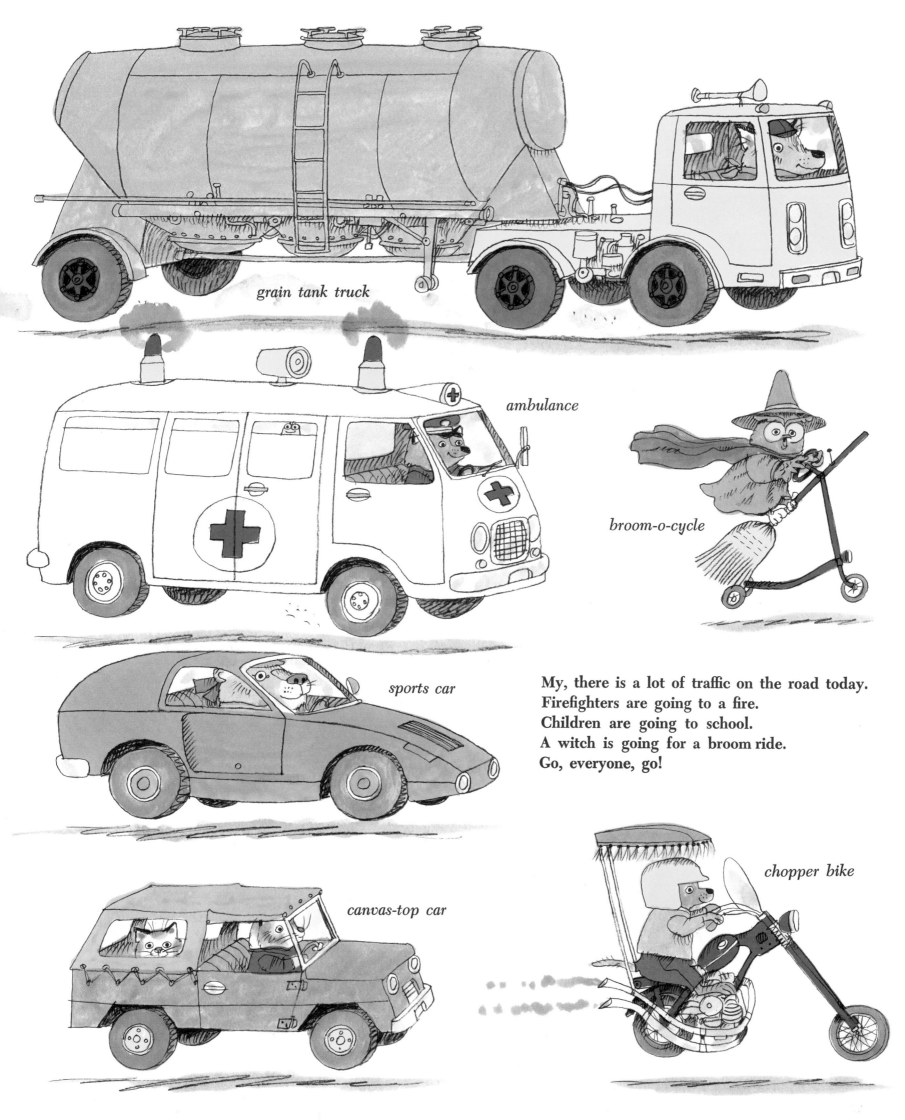

grain tank truck

ambulance

broom-o-cycle

sports car

My, there is a lot of traffic on the road today.
Firefighters are going to a fire.
Children are going to school.
A witch is going for a broom ride.
Go, everyone, go!

chopper bike

canvas-top car

big ditch-digger

Just look at all these machines!

Some dig ditches.
Some lay water pipes.

excavator

tiny ditch-digger

STOP

5-seater pencil car

auto transporter

street washer

64

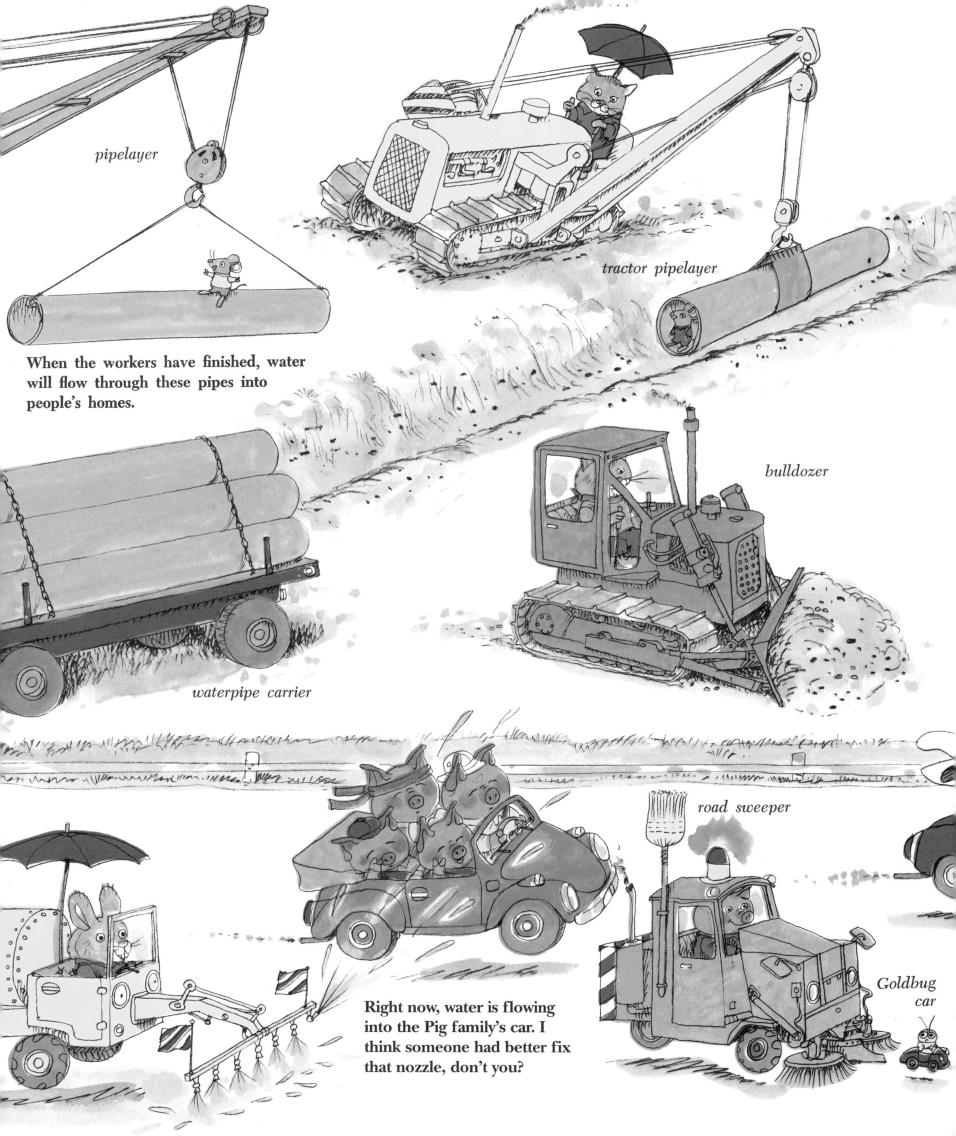

pipelayer

tractor pipelayer

When the workers have finished, water will flow through these pipes into people's homes.

bulldozer

waterpipe carrier

road sweeper

Right now, water is flowing into the Pig family's car. I think someone had better fix that nozzle, don't you?

Goldbug car

rock dump truck

coal dump truck

My word! What is happening here?
Mrs. Rabbit calls to Mr. Rabbit to tell him where she wants
him to dump the wheelbarrow. But Mr. Rabbit can't hear
her.
So Mrs. Rabbit shouts as loud as she can, so loud that all
the truckdrivers think she is shouting at them.

Goldbug
dump truck

orange dump truck

wheelbarrow

toy dump truck

cement dump truck

tomato dump truck

sand side-dump truck

"DUMP IT THERE!" she shouts . . . and all the drivers dump their loads right THERE!

double-decker bus

FUEL OIL

fuel oil tank truck

refrigerator van

ICE CREAM

Land-Rover

old-time coupe

another 5-seater pencil car

trailer truck

old-time
double-decker bus

BOOKS ARE
FUN TO READ

READ ONE TODAY

2-seater crayon car

TV
REPAIR

TV repair car

light bulb
pick-up truck

Well, the orange-truck driver has given Penny and Pickles
an orange.
"I'm glad it wasn't the coal truck that dumped on us,"
says Pickles.

hitchhiker

jeep

"Look there!" says Penny. "I wonder if anyone would have
enough room to pick up that hitchhiker."
I think he had better start walking, don't you?

awning

YOUR FRIENDLY CAR DEALER

HARDWARE

SALE on NAILS

new car

sidewalk

cement mixer

MISTRESS MOUSE REPAIRS

CROSS WALK

Now what?
Charlie the carpenter has just bought a bag of nails.
There was a hole in the bag.
Now there are holes in almost all the tires!

hammer car

USED CARS

used car

school bus

SCHOOL BUS

hard hat

flat tire

antique buggy

cherry picker

Where's Dingo? How did he manage to get by without a flat tire? I see Officer Flossy is riding on the sidewalk.
Keep after him, Flossy!
Hi, Goldbug . . . wherever you are.

STOP

trolley bus

bug bus

motor scooter

SIGHTSEEING TOURS

sightseeing bus

yellow
violet
orange
brown
red
blue
green
pink

PAUL THE PAINTER

a painter's pick-up truck

LIBRARY

sewer cleaner

ditch-digger

mobile crane

SQUEEZE LEFT
ROAD CONSTRUCTION
AHEAD

ant bus

hot dog car

rumble-seat roadster

coupe with open back hatch

Pa is all worn out from changing the tire. He is taking a nap in the backseat while Ma drives.

All right, everyone! Slow down! There is road construction ahead.

coupe with open sunroof

dump truck

Goldbugdozer

wheel loader

dumped-over dump truck

motor grader

SPEED LIMIT 15 MPH

The heavy roadwork machines scrape and push the dirt and rocks about, to make a smooth roadbed for a new road.

four antique sports cars
Count them!

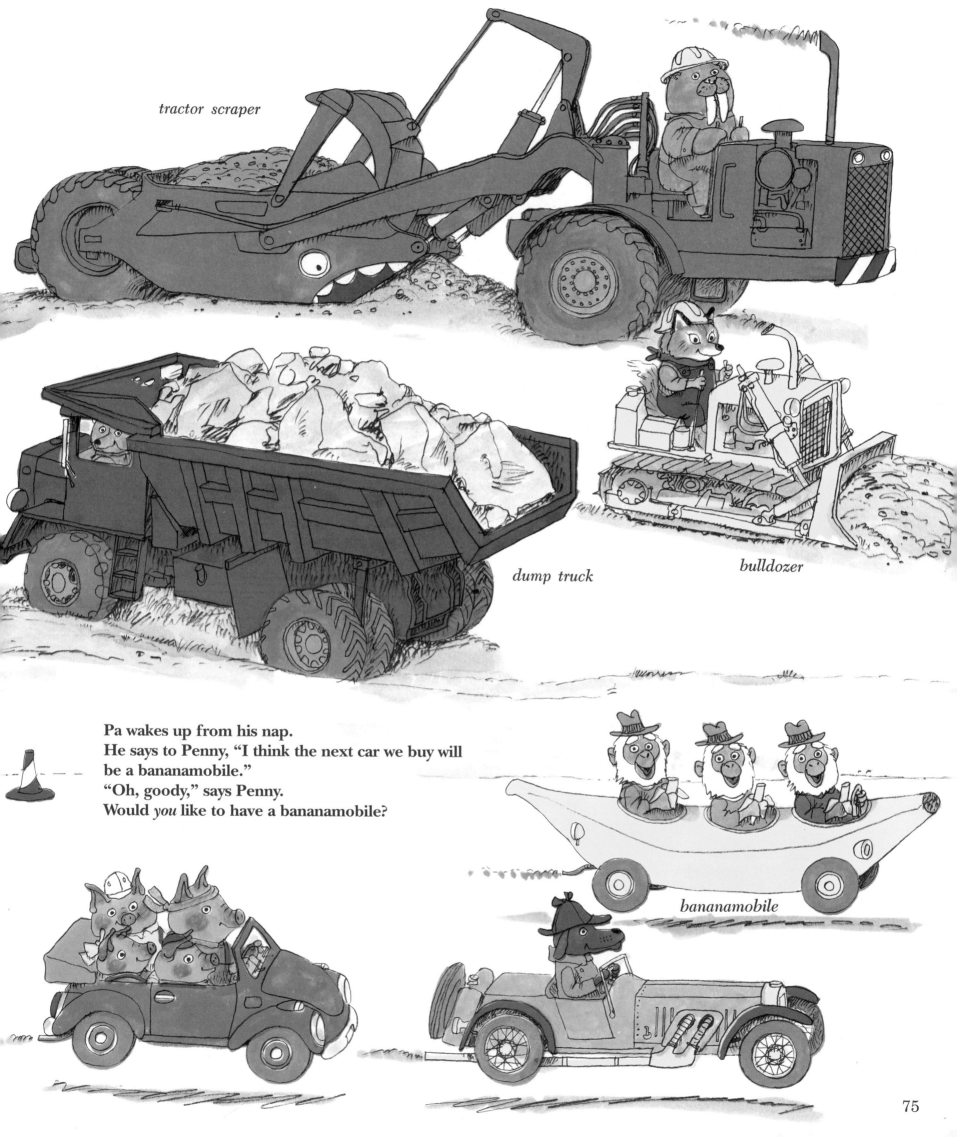

tractor scraper

dump truck

bulldozer

Pa wakes up from his nap.
He says to Penny, "I think the next car we buy will
be a bananamobile."
"Oh, goody," says Penny.
Would *you* like to have a bananamobile?

bananamobile

75

dumper
trailer

off-highway tractor

Mistress Mouse pumping up a flat tire

tractor loader

MISTRESS MOUSE REPAIRS

Why don't you watch what you're doing?

auto-digger

Here are more workers and more roadwork machines. Some workers are not watching what their machines are doing!

76

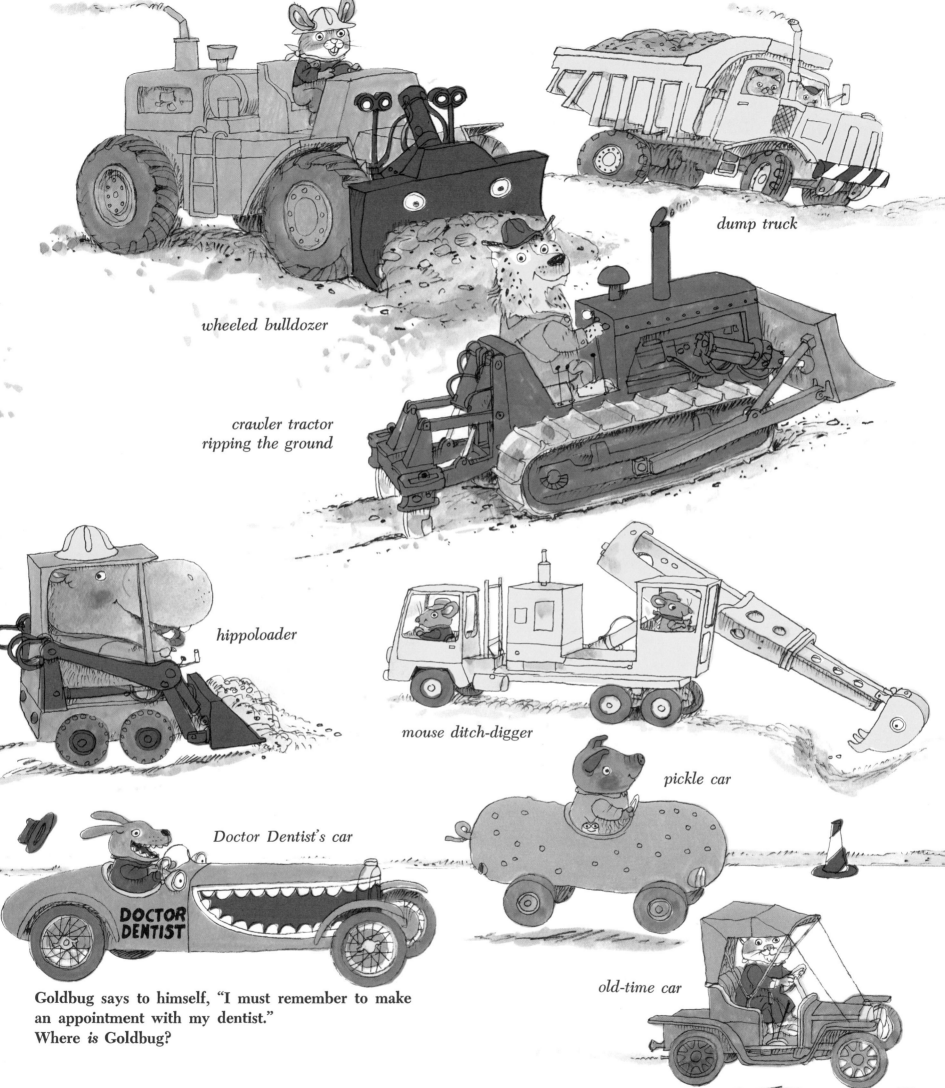

wheeled bulldozer

dump truck

crawler tractor
ripping the ground

hippoloader

mouse ditch-digger

pickle car

Doctor Dentist's car

old-time car

Goldbug says to himself, "I must remember to make
an appointment with my dentist."
Where *is* Goldbug?

77

power shovel

rock crusher

motor grader

tamper-downer

limousine

teeny-tiny
limousine

mini-limousine

sports car

78

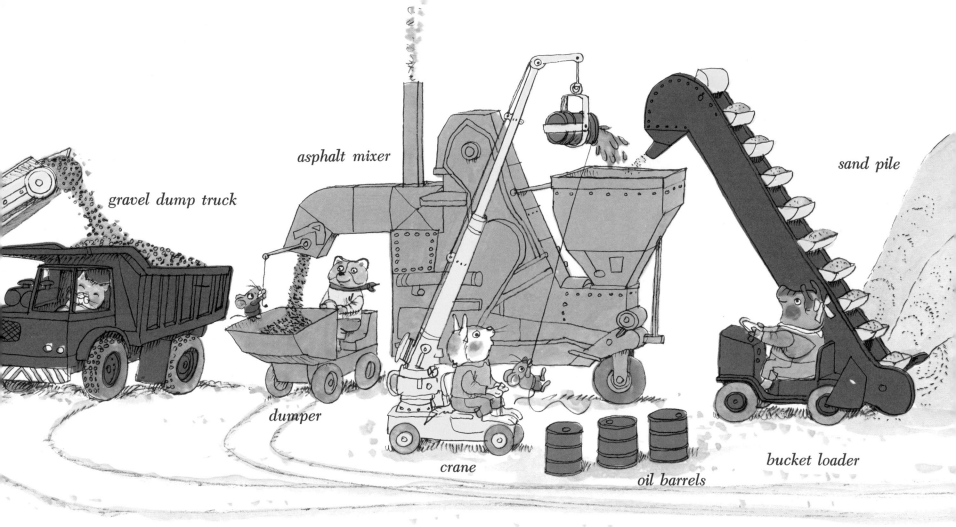

gravel dump truck

asphalt mixer

sand pile

dumper

crane

oil barrels

bucket loader

The roadbed is almost ready to be surfaced.
The rock crusher crushes big rocks into small stones.
Oil and sand are mixed together in the asphalt mixer and
out comes asphalt—hot, steaming asphalt.

taxi

carrotcar

"I think I would rather have
a carrotcar," says Pickles.

David Dog's car

79

gravel truck

asphalt oil spreader

stone spreader

custom buggy

Look out! Rollo Rabbit's steamroller has run away. Crunch! *CRUNCH!* CRUNCH! It has squashed three cars flat.

Look out, Flossy!
Look out, Mousie!
Look out, Ma!
Don't get squashed, too!

a runaway steamroller

STOP

guard rail

asphalt dumper

a sleepy
bear dozer

roller

asphalt road

asphalt finisher

a dumped
steamroller driver

Why don't you
look where
you're going?

three squashed cars
Count them!

OUCH!

Well, well. If it isn't our old
friend Dingo.
I think someone is after you,
Dingo!

TAXI

taxi

cheese car

81

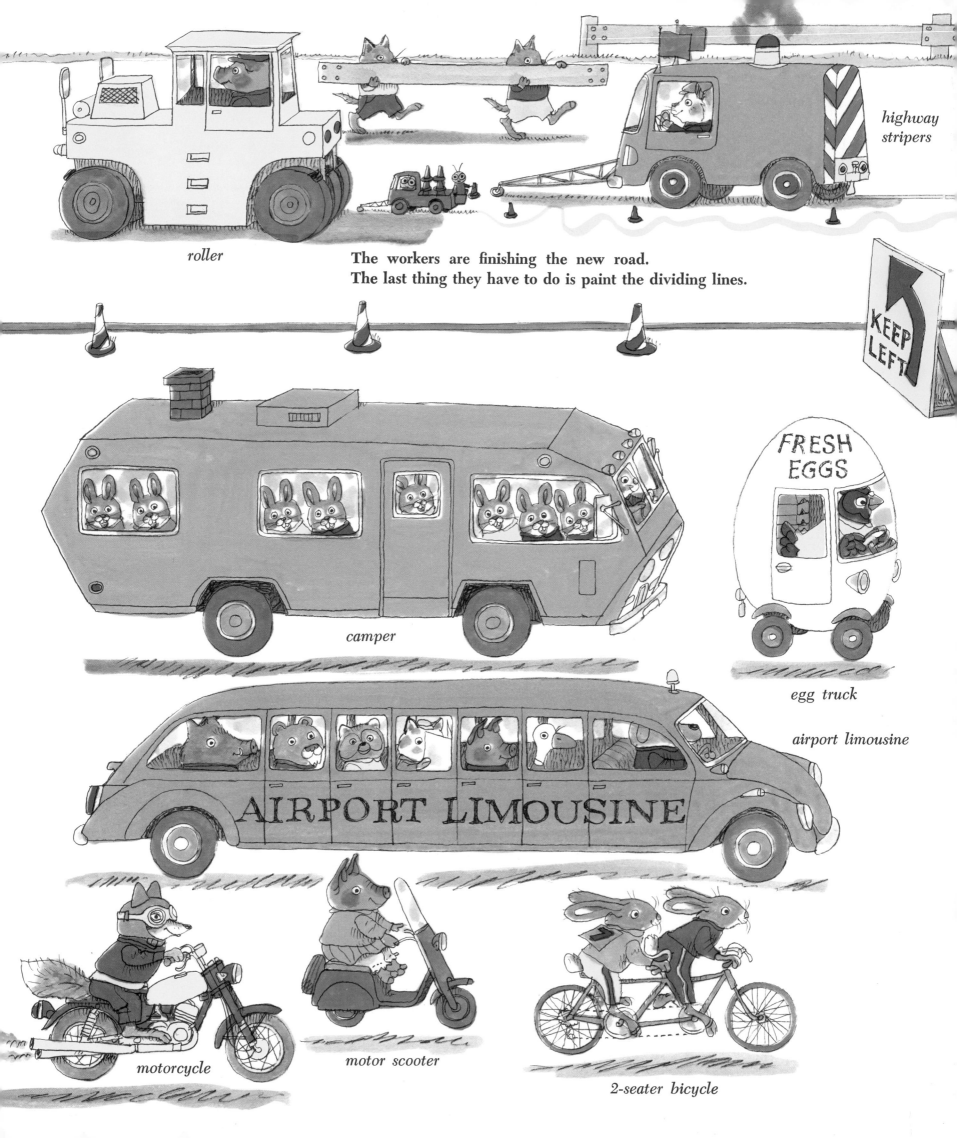

roller

highway stripers

The workers are finishing the new road.
The last thing they have to do is paint the dividing lines.

KEEP LEFT

FRESH EGGS

camper

egg truck

airport limousine

AIRPORT LIMOUSINE

motorcycle

motor scooter

2-seater bicycle

Maniacbug

Say! Who is that making a mess of the line? That's not Goldbug, is it?
No, it can't be Goldbug. He would never do a thing like that. That fellow must be Maniacbug.

sports roadster

bookshelf maker's car

Keep left, everyone. Drive slowly onto the new road.

farm tractor

a tired traveler

hay-and-pig wagon (Make a wish!)

mini-bus

antique car

toothbrush car

STOP

GAS

gasoline tank truck

GASOLINE

gas pump

hose

REST ROOMS

a woodchuck
in a hurry

car washer

CAR WASH

84

mini-jeep

old-time buggy

toothpaste car

EXIT

attendant

oil cans

Ma Pig sees that they are running low on gas, so she drives into the gas station to fill up the tank. I can find Goldbug, but I can't see the Pig family. Where do you suppose they have gone?

dirty station wagon

auto lift

car greaser

85

hook-and-ladder truck

rescue truck

ALL RIGHT!
Who left the water
running in that
fire engine?

water tower truck

fire alarm box

siren

hose

Fire Chief's car

CHIEF

The Pig family is all refreshed. The gas tank is full again, and Pa is back at the wheel.

nozzle

ambulance

Ladybug has a fire in her car and the fire fighters have come to put it out.
Can you guess who called them?

bell

helmet

pumper truck

fire hydrant 87

diesel locomotive

mail car

tank car

boxcar

forklift

All the wheels need to be oiled so they won't squeak. Squeaky Mouse says so.

Tom Turtle's car

antique car

gardener's truck

88

auto carrier car

double-decker coach car

steam locomotive

1½   1½

railroad station

CLOVER

station wagon

THIS SIDE UP

doughnut car

DOUGHNUTS

Railroad stations are busy places. There are always lots of people coming and going. Freight trains load and unload letters, food, packages, and all sorts of things.

Some people like to go far away for their vacation. If they want to have their car to drive, they can take it along on the train's auto carrier car.

"I hope I remembered to put doughnuts in the picnic basket," Ma says to herself.
I wonder what made her think of that?

STOP

racing cars

bigshot car

canvas-roof car

old-time racing car

pick-up truck

MR. GREEN THUMB GARDENER

"Look," says Penny, "an auto race!"
"I'm too hungry to look," says Pickles.
"Now just be patient," says Ma. "It won't be long before we have our picnic. But first we must stop at Grandma Pig's farm and buy some fresh corn."

VAROOM! VAROOM!
VAROOM!
And the winner is . . .
MISTRESS MOUSE!

mouse-car transporter

rhinoceros car

sunroof car

91

corn picker

hay gatherer

At Grandma Pig's farm, all the farmhands are very busy.
They are picking corn, gathering hay, and delivering milk.
They are harvesting wheat to be made into bread.
Grandpa is cutting the grass and Grandma is clanking
around on her old steam tractor.
My! What a busy farm!

milk cans

corn car

Auntie Pastry and Cousin Willie are selling fresh corn.
It looks so good, Pa just has to take a bite.
"No, Pa," says Ma. "Don't eat it yet! Wait until I cook it!"

well

FRESH
CORN

wheat

grain harvester

tractor

Grandma's steam tractor

grass cutter

Wolfwagon

93

swimming tank

landing craft

swimming jeep

desert jeep

motorcycle and sidecar

tractor motorcycle

General Nuisance's car

water jeep

jeep

half-track soldier carrier

bridge

Won't you please wake up, Mister Soldier?

tent

The Pigs have bought their corn and are on the way to the beach for their picnic. They are passing an army camp. Look at all the soldiers!

94

chapel truck

canteen truck

radio truck

old-time tank

ambulance

antique armored car

tank

army car

gun tractor

These soldiers are going home for the weekend to visit their families. Their car is just like an army car, but it is painted differently.

civilian car

95

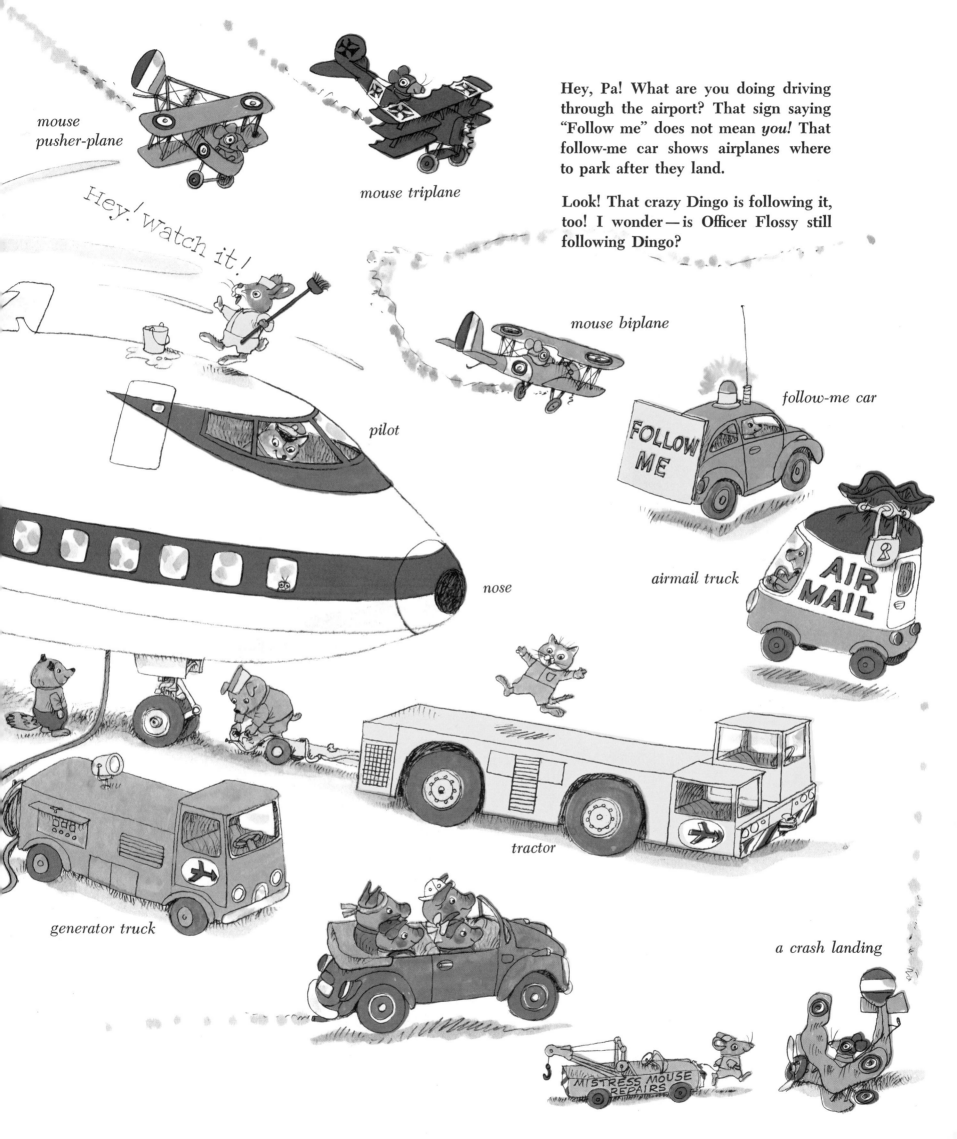

mouse pusher-plane

mouse triplane

Hey! watch it!

mouse biplane

pilot

nose

follow-me car

FOLLOW ME

airmail truck

AIR MAIL

Hey, Pa! What are you doing driving through the airport? That sign saying "Follow me" does not mean *you*! That follow-me car shows airplanes where to park after they land.

Look! That crazy Dingo is following it, too! I wonder—is Officer Flossy still following Dingo?

generator truck

tractor

a crash landing

MISTRESS MOUSE REPAIRS

mobile apartment house

sun-roof camper

mobile home

Kitty camper

roof-bed camper

grill with two burned hot dogs

"I do hope we get to the beach soon," says Pa.

trailer home

old-school-bus home

swimming-pool truck

just-a-little-bit-too-small camper

The Hogs are spending their vacation at a trailer camp. "We don't seem to be able to get through the gate," Mama Hog says to Papa Hog. "I wonder if we should leave a few things at home next year?"

HAPPY HOURS CAMP

HOG HEAVEN

PLEASE WIPE FEET

NO RIDERS

There's Officer Flossy! Go get him, Flossy!

shark car

ICE CREAM

ice-cream truck

sand dune

mouse dune buggy

sand boat

Oh, Piggy, you made a mistake!
Your car won't run in the water.
Only a propeller car can do that.

propeller car

surrey car

BATH HOUSE

shower

refreshment stand

dune buggies

Roll bars protect
the driver in case
the buggy rolls over.

"AT LAST!" says Ma. "We are at the
beach and we are going to have a nice
quiet picnic. Pa, maybe you should put
a shirt on. I think you are getting
sunburned."
"Oh, I'll be all right," says Pa.

go-anywhere buggy

pedal boat

submarine

101

forklift

The picnic is over, and Pa is not all right.
He is all RED! WOW! What a sunburn!
Pa is also all stuffed, with food. A nap is
just what he needs, so Ma drives for a while.
Close your mouth when you sleep, Pa!

dock

propeller

tugboat

air-cushion ferry (hovercraft)

FERRY

FERRY

TICKET
OFFICE

crane

flag

radar

smokestack

lifeboat

a furious captain

anchor

cargo freighter

a falling car

tender car

barge

straddle truck

Pa is missing all the sights of the harbor. Cars are being
loaded onto a freighter, to be carried across the ocean
to far parts of the world.
Oh, my! One of them is not going any farther than the
bottom of the harbor!

flying fish

FISH

fish truck

garbage truck

9

WATCH WHAT YOU'RE DOING!!

squasher-downer

bulldozer

a squashed-down golf cart

Two golfers have lost their golf
balls in the garbage dump.
Please help find them.

TOWN
DUMP

caterpillar bus

cross-country car

104

The Pig family is driving up into the mountains. It is getting colder. It is snowing. The road is icy. The pie truck skids off the road.
Mistress Mouse says it is time to put on snow chains. Hey Pa! Wake up! Put on your snow chains! And please put the top up.

a skidding pie truck

icy road

SLIPPERY WHEN WET

bent sign

MISTRESS MOUSE REPAIRS

a worker stringing wire on telephone poles

MOM'S PIES

TELEPHONE COMPANY

spool of wire

telephone truck

snow bus

Ma put on the snow chains.
Ma put the top up.
WOW! Just look at all that snow! Isn't it beautiful?
There's a pile of things all covered with snow on the truck
behind the Pigs. I wonder what they could be?

Harry, dear!
You must remember
to close the
window
after you!

snowplow

sled

106

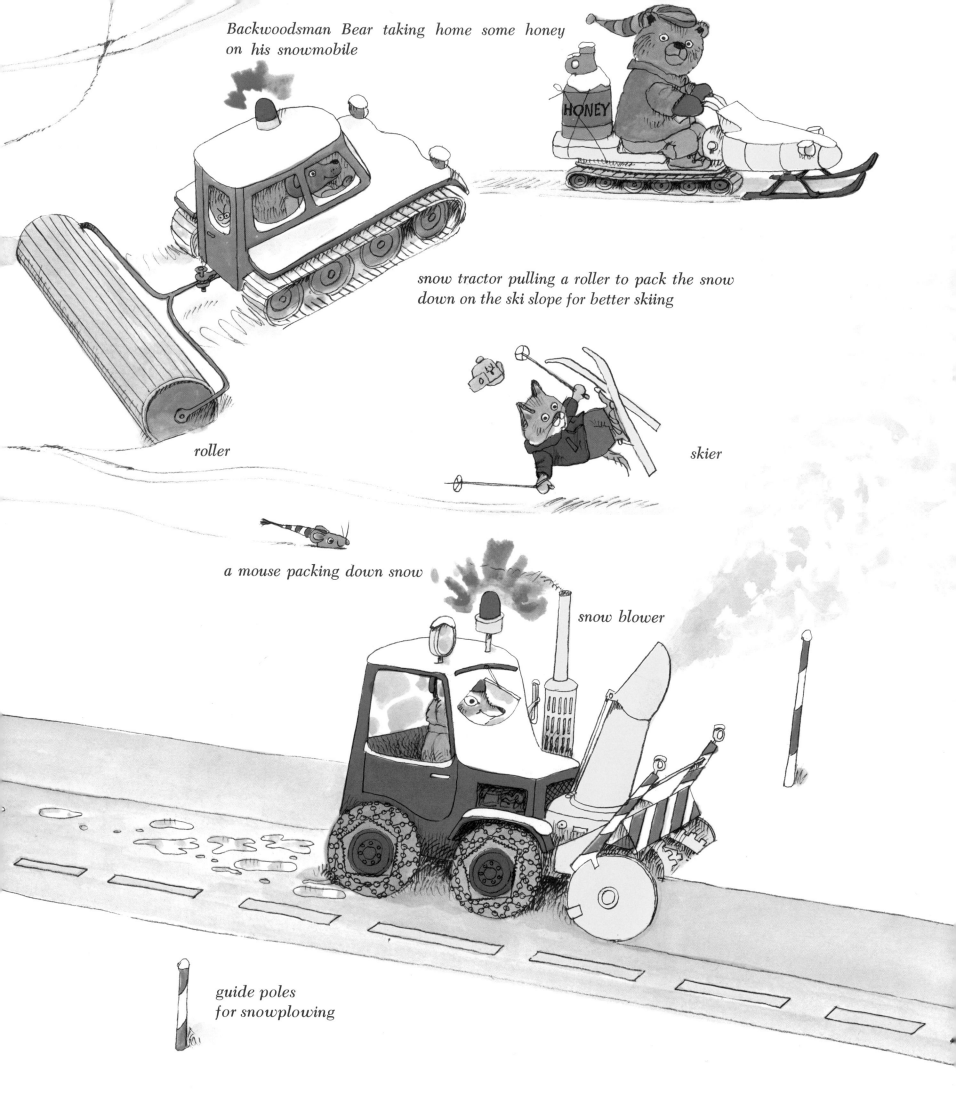

Backwoodsman Bear taking home some honey on his snowmobile

snow tractor pulling a roller to pack the snow down on the ski slope for better skiing

roller

skier

a mouse packing down snow

snow blower

guide poles for snowplowing

express truck
and trailers

EXPRESS 1

tipped-over
watermelon truck

STOP!

Did you guess what those things are, all covered
with snow?
Well! Now you KNOW! They are watermelons.
STOP, WATERMELONS, STOP!

Henry, chasing a watermelon

antique car

cement mixer

The noise of the rolling watermelons awakens Pa.
Ma stops and Pa takes off the snow chains.
They have come down out of the mountains, and
there is no more snow.
Now Ma is helping Pa put the top down, as the
snow is all melted . . . well, *almost* all melted.

snow chains

runaway watermelons

EXPRESS 2

EXPRESS 3

STOP

chemical
tank truck

mountain
climber

Harry, chasing
a watermelon

STOP!

Carl Cat's car

roadster

skis on a rack

snowshoe

SKI SCHOOL

ski-school bus

Oh, NO!
I never thought I would see an accident
as bad as this one! This is what I would
call SOME ACCIDENT!
It just doesn't seem possible, does it?
But there you are ... you can see
for yourself.
And poor Mistress Mouse! It will
probably take her a MILLION YEARS
to fix everything.
Luckily, no one was badly hurt.

WHIPPED CREAM

FIRE DE

FLOUR

TOMATO JUICE

BANANAS

FRESH EGGS

MISTRESS MOUSE REPAIRS

The egg men always wear seat belts so that they
won't fall out and get broken. Do you?

"Well, we are almost home now," says Pa.
"Thank goodness," says Ma.

And, sure enough, here they are.
"BACK, SAFE, HOME AGAIN," they all say together.
In front of their house, a delivery man is just leaving.
"What are those boxes on the front lawn?" asks Ma.
"What are those boxes on the front lawn?" asks Penny.
"What are those boxes on the front lawn?" asks Pickles.
Pa just smiles and doesn't ask anything.
"Oh, look!" says Ma. "I think we are going to have new neighbors."

delivery van

mobile library

advertising car

electrician's van

SOLD

Take care, Mr Loving

THE 3 MOVERS

TENDER, LOVING, AND CARE

moving van

battery-powered car

ADAM'S APPLES

apple van

WE PRESS SUITS WHILE U WAIT

You missed a wrinkle, Joe!

steamroller

And, sure enough, Ma is right, as usual. They *do* have new neighbors.
And Penny and Pickles — and Goldbug, too! — have new automobiles!
Pa bought them at the toy shop at the start of their trip.
Do you remember his visit to the toy shop?

Hi! Hi! Hi! Hi! Hi! Hi! Hi! Hi! Hi! Hi! Hi! Hi! Hi! Hi! Hi! Hi! Hi! Hi! Hi! Hi! Hi! Hi!

F.D.

POLICE

7

STOP

Yikes!

Well, at last! Officer Flossy has finally caught that Dingo. When will he ever learn to drive properly? Probably never...but we can always hope for the best. My! Hasn't it been an exciting day?

THIS IS THE END

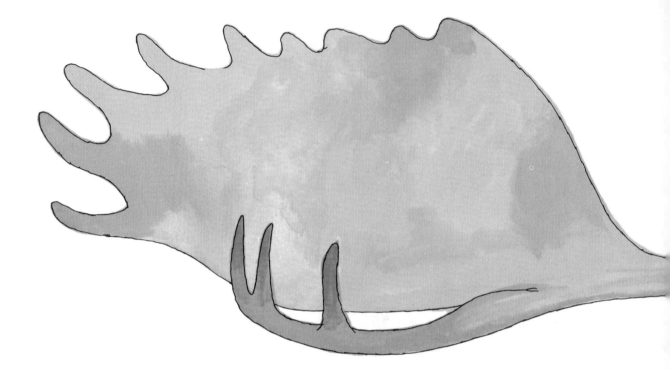

mosquito

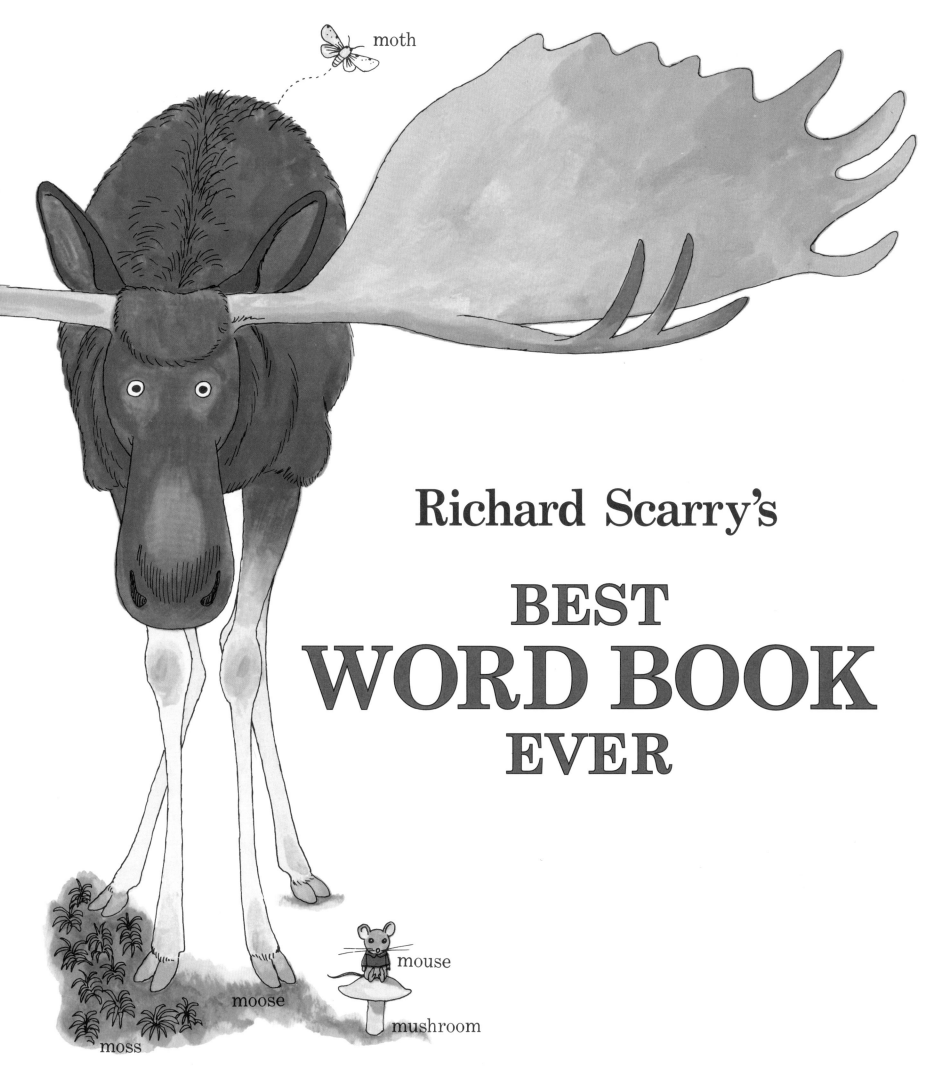

moth

Richard Scarry's

BEST
WORD BOOK
EVER

mouse

moose

mushroom

moss

curtains

sun

window

THE NEW DAY

It is the morning of a new day.
The sun is shining.
Kenny Bear gets up out of bed.

washcloth

soap

towel

First he washes his
face and hands.

toothbrush

toothpaste

Then he brushes
his teeth.

comb

mirror

pajamas

He combs his hair.

shirt

pants

He dresses himself.

He makes his bed.

He goes to the kitchen
to eat his breakfast.

118

Kenny Bear sits in
his favorite chair.

He is very hungry.
This is what he eats—

cold fruit juice

warm cereal

with cream

pancakes

with butter and maple syrup

He doesn't eat
the toaster.

fried eggs

bacon

toast

muffins

honey

jam

hot cocoa

cool milk

and a waffle.

When he finishes eating breakfast he helps
wash and dry the dishes.

cup   saucer   plate   bowl   fork   knife   spoon   glass

jar   pitcher   frying pan   lid   pot   pan   bottle   juice squeezer   glass

Now he is ready to play with his friends.

119

THE RABBIT FAMILY'S HOUSE

Father Rabbit, Mother Rabbit, and the Rabbit children are getting ready for the new day. Their friend Owl is waiting for the children to come outside. Can you find him?

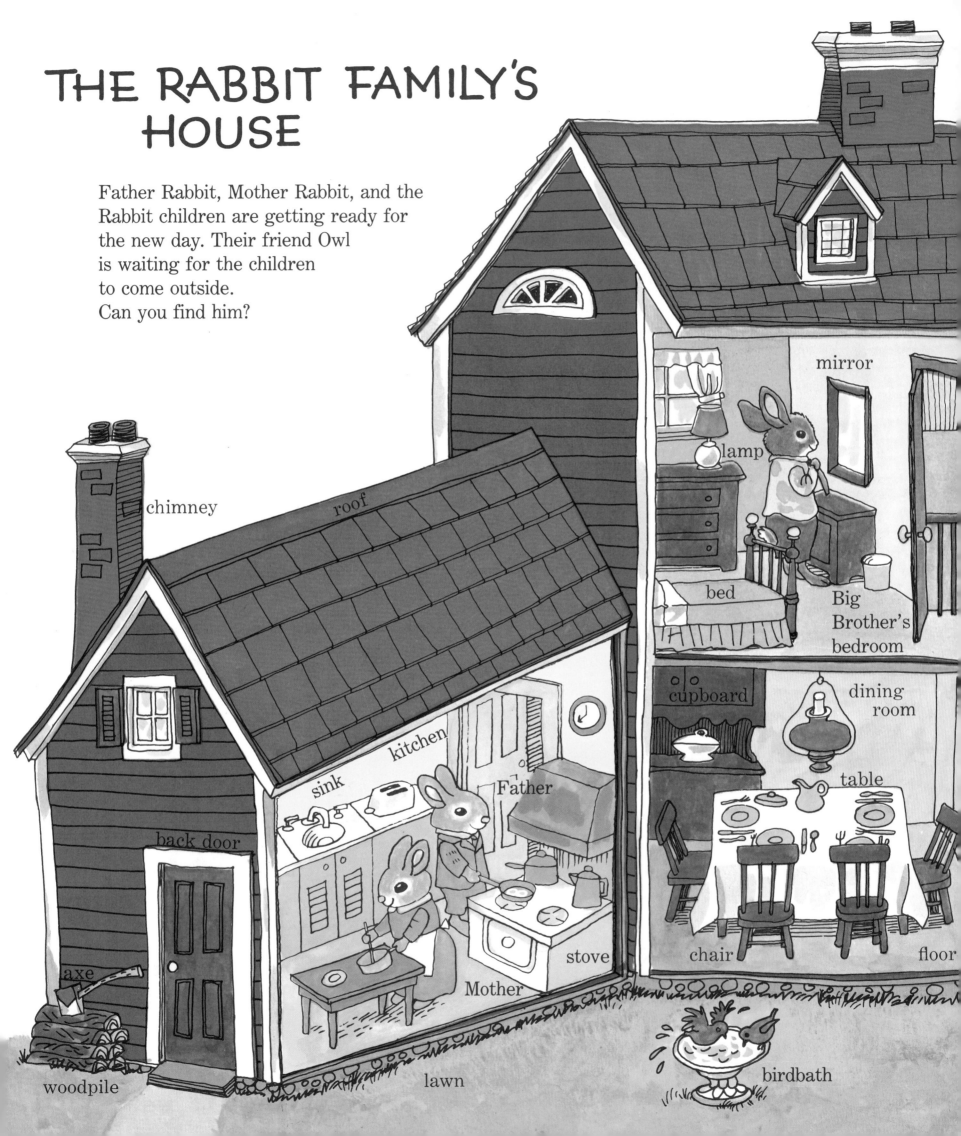

chimney

roof

mirror

lamp

bed

Big Brother's bedroom

cupboard

dining room

kitchen

sink

Father

table

back door

stove

chair

floor

axe

Mother

woodpile

lawn

birdbath

WHOO
owl

smoke

antenna

light
switch

television set

record player

hassock

Mickey

bunk bed

Molly

bathroom

upstairs hall

bedroom

front door

living room

outside
light

candle

picture

telephone

fireplace

stairs

sofa or couch

front
hall

doormat

rug

window

stone walk

121

PAINTING AND DRAWING WITH COLORS

Painting and drawing are fun.
You can use bright colors.
You can paint with brushes
or even your fingers. You can
draw with crayons or pencils.
What do you like to draw?

paper

finger painting

make orange

make green

pencil

eraser

pencil drawing

make violet

make pink

make gray

make brown

water dish

watercolors

poster paint

smock

paintbrushes

crayons

pastels

122

TOYS

Sometimes it is fun to play by yourself. Sometimes it is fun to play with your friends. What are your favorite toys? Do you like to play with blocks?

rocking horse

tricycle

electric trains

truck and loader

blocks

scooter

glider

robot

building set

croquet

AT THE PLAYGROUND

The children are all having fun doing
different things. Which children are
doing the things you like best?

seesaw

leapfrog

hide-and-seek

slide

somersault

ring-around-a-rosie

jump rope

ladder

rings

swing

sliding pole

top

roller skates

bubble blowing

kite

jungle gym

merry-go-round

tag

ring toss

hoop rolling

jacks

marbles

sandbox

kite string

bouncing ball

hopscotch

125

hammer

nail

TOOLS

Everyone is very busy
working with tools.
What tools do you have
in your house? What
would you like to build?

pushpin

axe

carpenter

ladder

board

sandpaper

log

saw

sawdust

hacksaw

drill

vise

plane

woodpecker

jigsaw

wood shavings

screwdriver

screws

pliers

file

126

bucksaw

trowel

bricklayer

hoe

brick wall

cement

brick

lumber

fence painter

paintbrush

ball of twine

sawhorse

barrel

paint

tack

tack hammer

hatchet

ruler

folding ruler

toolbox

jackknife

square

putty knife

shovel

bolt

nut

dirt

monkey wrench

compass

wheelbarrow

pickaxe

glue

crow

scarecrow

weather vane

silo

disc harrow

field

tractor

N
W E
S

barn

hayloft

goat

stall

tin can

milk can

pail

farm truck

wagon

hen

rooster

pigsty

baby chick

Kathy Bear is going
to feed the pig.

corncrib

haystack

cow

apple tree

farmhouse

water pump

meadow

fence

sheep

horse

apple

grass

clothesline

clothes basket

THE BEARS' FARM

Kenny Bear is going
to feed the chickens.

The Bears are working hard on their farm.
What are they all doing? What is the duck doing?
What is the scarecrow supposed to be doing?
He is not doing it, is he?

chicken coop

mailbox

well

duck pond

duck   ducklings

bee

pitchfork

beehive

129

weather instruments

blimp

microphone

control tower

AT THE AIRPORT

The air traffic controller is talking to the pilot of the jet passenger plane. The controller is giving the pilot take-off instructions.

baggage train

waiting room

binoculars

tourist

camera

observation deck

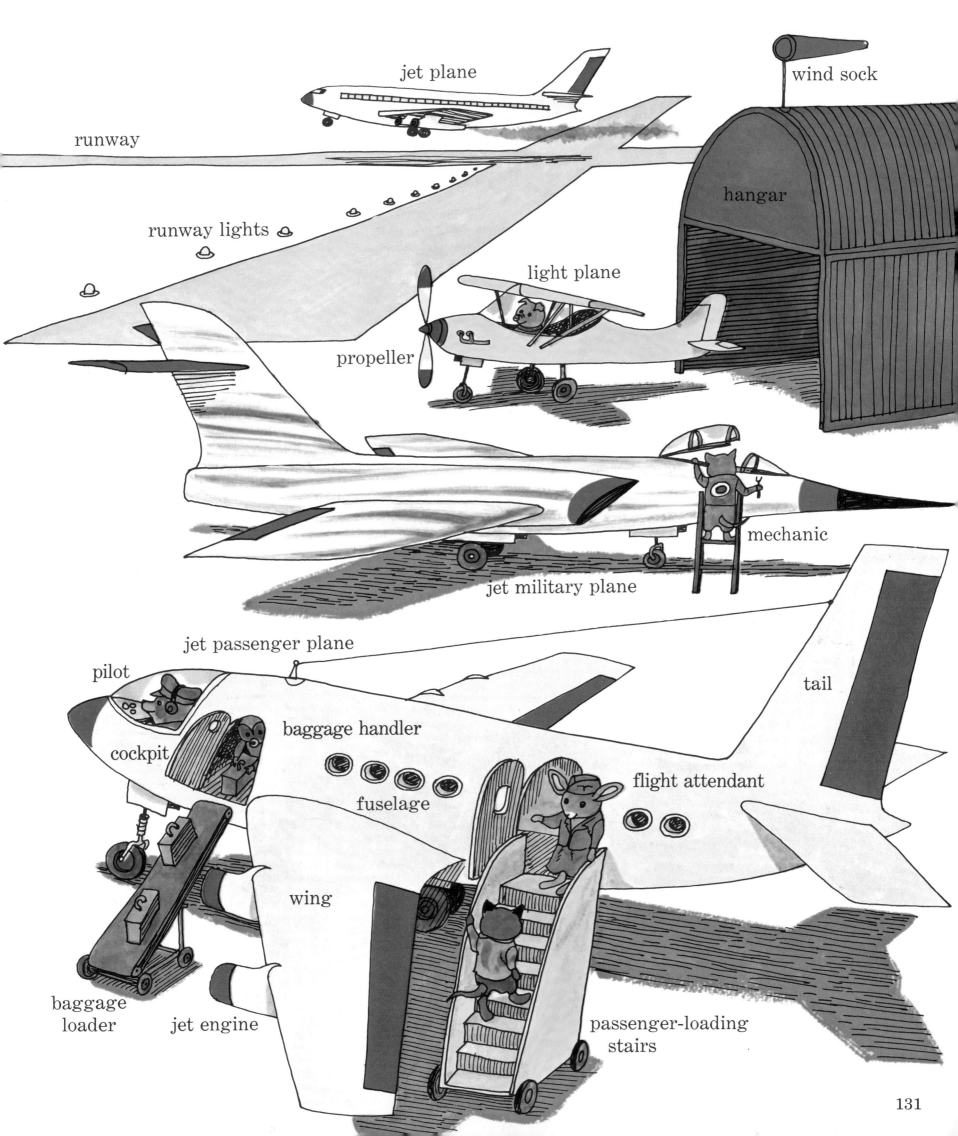

jet plane

wind sock

runway

hangar

runway lights

light plane

propeller

mechanic

jet military plane

jet passenger plane

pilot

tail

baggage handler

cockpit

flight attendant

fuselage

wing

baggage
loader

jet engine

passenger-loading
stairs

131

meat cleaver

hook

ham

saw

scales

MEATS

wrapping paper

twine

pickle barrel

butcher

garbage pail

bologna

frankfurters

hamburger

bacon

chop

fish

steak

a piglet who wants to work in the supermarket when she grows up

cart

sawdust

AT THE SUPERMARKET

The Pigs are buying groceries for their family. What would you like to buy next time you go to the market? Would you like to buy a pickle?

books

GOLDEN BOOKS

customer

shopper

orange juice

raisins

money

purse

cashier

eggs

milk

butter

ice cream

cash register

FRUITS

pineapple

bananas

scales

grocer

apples

oranges

pears

grapefruit

melons

grapes

lemons

cherries

strawberries

raspberries

blueberries

plums

peaches

watermelon

coconut

pumpkin

VEGETABLES

corn

beans

lettuce

tomatoes

peas

cabbage

asparagus

celery

spinach

potatoes

squash

beets

onions

cauliflower

carrots

cucumbers

turnip

broom

cookies

sugar

cereal

spaghetti

canned food

peanut butter

cheese

salt

apricots

baby food

bread

jam

MEALTIME

The Pig family is having a special holiday meal. There is so much good food to enjoy! What do you see on the table that you like to eat?

carving knife and fork

roast beef

meat platter

tablespoon

coffeepot

teapot

saltshaker

pepper shaker

fork

dinner plate

glass

cream pitcher

knife

spoon

cup

saucer

sugar bowl

napkin

turkey

cake

milk pitcher

green beans

gelatine

cranberry sauce

baked potatoes

squash

mashed potatoes

onions

beets

ice cream

peas

steak

butter

soup

pie

salad

white bread

rye bread

rolls

135

smokestack

submarine

stern

ocean liner

bow

police boat

POLICE

barge

tugboat

ferryboat

pirate ship

BOATS AND SHIPS

One of the things in the water is not a boat, but it helps boats find the place they want to go. Do you know what it is?

motorboat

paddle   canoe

kayak

oar   rowboat

freighter

lightship

AMBROSE

coast guard ship

CG-7

oil tanker

fireboat

F.D.

fishing
nets

fishing trawler

sport-fishing boat

speedboat

10

houseboat

raft

THE WHITE SWAN

sailboat

light buoy

2

KEEPING HEALTHY

Your doctors and your dentist are your good friends. They want you to stay healthy and strong. Will you give your doctors and dentist a big smile the next time you see them? How big a smile can you smile?

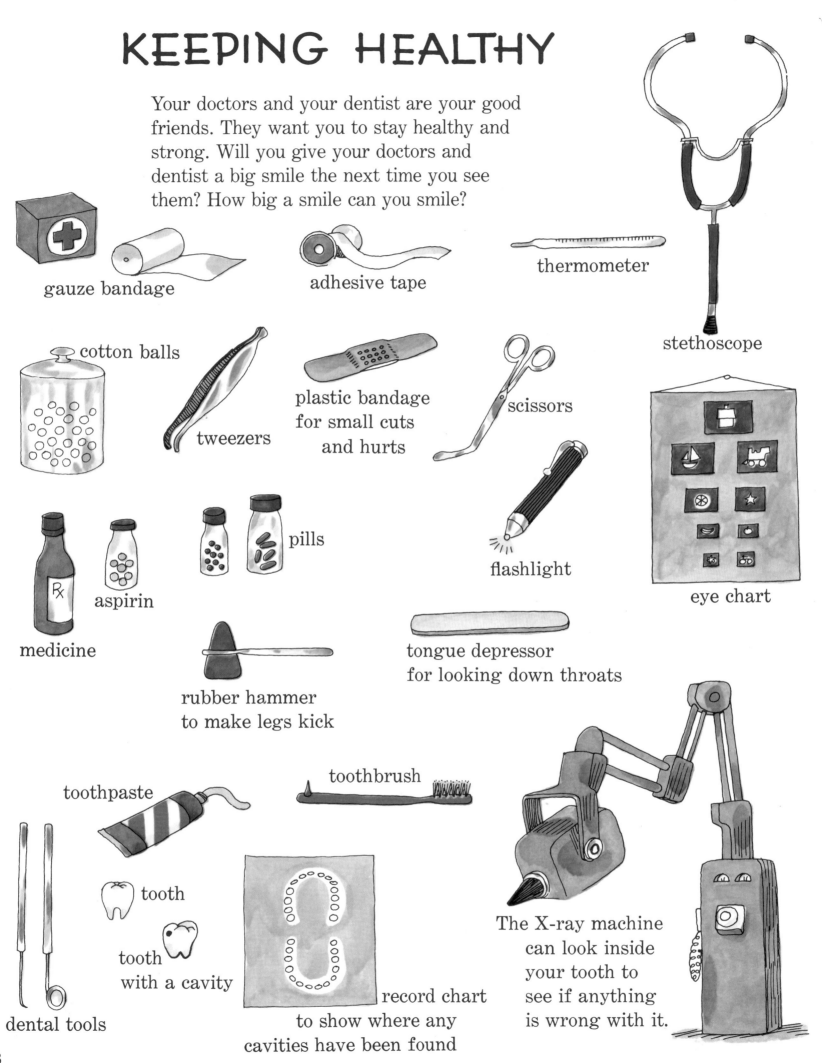

gauze bandage

adhesive tape

thermometer

stethoscope

cotton balls

tweezers

plastic bandage for small cuts and hurts

scissors

flashlight

eye chart

aspirin

pills

medicine

rubber hammer to make legs kick

tongue depressor for looking down throats

toothpaste

toothbrush

tooth

tooth with a cavity

dental tools

record chart to show where any cavities have been found

The X-ray machine can look inside your tooth to see if anything is wrong with it.

The doctor listens to your heart.

scales

hurt tail

doctor

patient

eye doctor

The eye doctor
tests your eyes.

dental
engine

dentist

rinse
bowl

instrument table

water cup

dentist's chair

dental unit

dental hygienist

The dentist looks for cavities and the dental
hygienist explains how to care for your teeth.

THE BEAR TWINS GET DRESSED

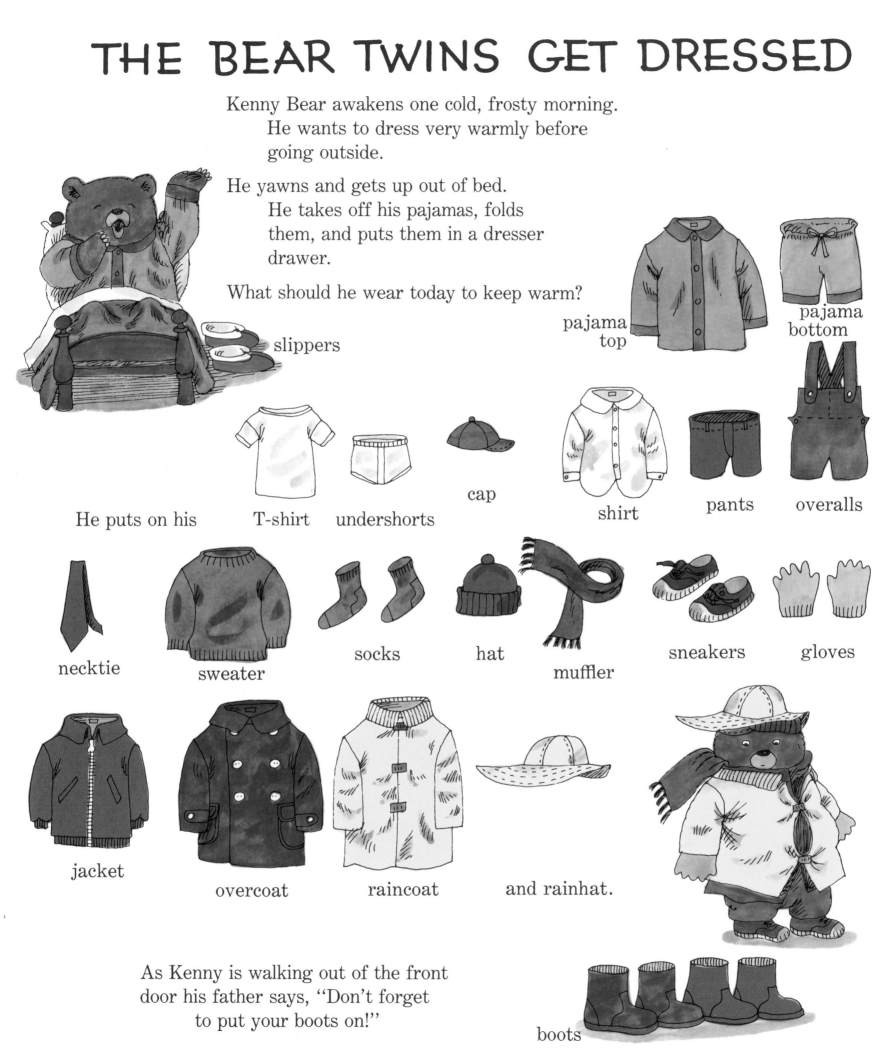

Kenny Bear awakens one cold, frosty morning. He wants to dress very warmly before going outside.

He yawns and gets up out of bed. He takes off his pajamas, folds them, and puts them in a dresser drawer.

What should he wear today to keep warm?

slippers

pajama top

pajama bottom

He puts on his   T-shirt   undershorts   cap   shirt   pants   overalls

necktie   sweater   socks   hat   muffler   sneakers   gloves

jacket   overcoat   raincoat   and rainhat.

As Kenny is walking out of the front door his father says, "Don't forget to put your boots on!"

boots

140

Kathy Bear stretches hard before she gets out of bed. She takes off her nightgown and hangs it on the hook in her closet.

What do you think Kathy should wear today to keep warm?

nightgown

She puts on her

underpants

undershirt

hair ribbon

blouse

skirt

sweater

kneesocks

ear muffs

shoes

snowsuit

and mittens.

She puts her change purse

into her backpack.

As Kathy is walking out of the front door her mother says, "Don't forget to put your boots on!"

Do you ever forget to put on your boots?

141

deer

lion

elephant

tiger

panda

monkeys

brown bear

gorilla

polar bear

142

buffalo

camel

zebra

zookeeper

giraffe

leopard

sea lion

zoo train

The veterinarian
makes sure all the
animals are healthy.

AT THE ZOO

Mr. and Mrs. Mouse took
their children to the zoo.
How will those children
ever be able to get
all those balloons
into their house tonight?
Which is your favorite animal
at the zoo?

rhinoceros

balloon seller

hippopotamus

IN THE CITY

Mouse has just bought a book at the bookstore.
She is going to buy a newspaper and then join
her rabbit friends at the sidewalk cafe and drink some
lemonade with them. Show with your finger the way
she will go. Remember to have her look both
ways before she crosses a street.

144

hotel

street sign

park

park bench

statue

manhole

taxi

barbershop

sidewalk cafe

delivery cycle

traffic officer

police car

RESTAURANT

DANGER

one way

Miss CAT

THEATER

NOW PLAYING

TAXI STAND

BUS STOP

SUBWAY

bus

sidewalk

token seller

subway entrance

newspapers

newsstand

subway station

radio tower

A DRIVE
IN THE COUNTRY

There are many things to see when you take a drive
in the country. Can you see Harry and Sally,
the mountain climbers? Can you see what Harry
has dropped from his knapsack?

ocean

island

factory

lake

gas
station

tunnel

gas pump

tollbooth

turnpike or thruway
or superhighway

farm

bridge

mill

brook

stream

waterfall

picnic area

picnickers

lighthouse

beach

fire lookout tower

bay

crane

woods

drawbridge

seaport

hill

village

tug

mountain

windmill

river

pond

log cabin

mountain climbers

road

forest

knapsack

cliff

apple

HOLIDAYS

Holidays are happy times, aren't they?
Which holiday do you like best?
I bet you like them all.

On holidays we visit friends and relatives.
Sometimes we give or get presents.
What would you like to get for your birthday?

horn

New Year's Day

valentine

St. Valentine's Day

Easter

Easter egg

Easter bunny

Easter chick

balloons

rattle

cake   ice cream

Birthday

National Holiday

fireworks

flag

bugle

bass drum

fife

drum

uniform

ghost

Halloween

moon

witch

black cat

skeleton

witch's broom

pumpkin

Chanukah

trick-or-treat bag

angel

menorah

candle

wreath

Christmas

Christmas tree

holly

ornaments

stockings

tree lights

beard

fireplace

Santa Claus

bag

present

149

AT SCHOOL

School is fun. There are so many things we learn to do. Kathy Bear is learning how to find a lost mitten.

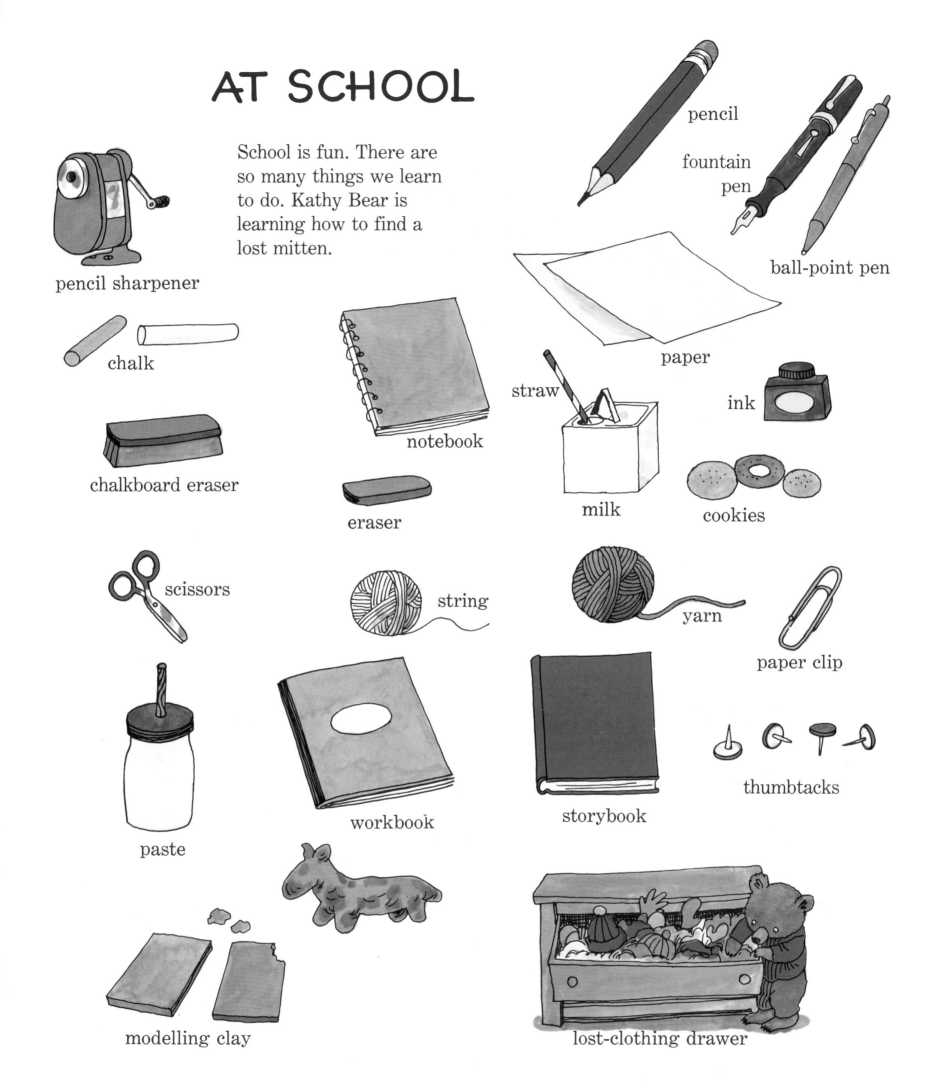

pencil

fountain pen

ball-point pen

pencil sharpener

chalk

chalkboard eraser

notebook

eraser

paper

straw

milk

ink

cookies

scissors

string

yarn

paper clip

paste

workbook

storybook

thumbtacks

modelling clay

lost-clothing drawer

flag

clock

bell

chalkboard

calendar

teacher

JANUARY

a b c

cat dog

inkwell

map

map stand

wastebasket

artist

pupil

desk

classroom

music teacher

paper shapes

refrigerator

kitchen cabinet

doorknob

can opener

soap

teapot

electrical outlet

counter

freezer

garbage pail

washing machine

dishwasher

Father Pig

laundry basket

eggbeater

eggshell

stool

Annie Pig

mixing bowl

batter
spoon

measuring cup

rolling pin

Susan
Pig

cookie cutter

dough

strainer

Peter
Pig

cake pan

funnel

cookie tray

ketchup
bottle

spatula

food grinder

flour bin

sugar bowl

mustard jar

closet

feather duster

broom

dustpan

mop

vacuum cleaner

egg timer

shelf

flyswatter

Mother Pig

hood

coffeepot

teakettle

burner

oven

stove

iron

ironing board

IN THE KITCHEN

All the Pigs like to work in the kitchen.
They are making good things to eat.
What is Father Pig making? What is
Mother Pig putting into the oven?

teaspoon

tablespoon

soup spoon

double boiler

blender

pestle

toaster

mortar

saucepan

corkscrew

ladle

colander

cutting board

measuring spoons

matches

potato masher

saltshaker

pepper grinder

cookbook

carving fork and knife

electric mixer

WHEN YOU GROW UP

What would you like to be when you are
bigger? Would you like to be a good
cook like your father? Would you like
to be a doctor or a nurse?

What would you like to be?

police officer

fire fighter

sailor

nurse

taxi driver

farmer

gardener

doctor

carpenter

musician

scientist

baker

dentist

secretary

good cook

singer

artist

pilot

fisherman

truck driver

teacher

garage mechanic

reporter

photographer

storekeeper

judge

librarian

dancer

daddy

mommy

155

THINGS WE DO

There are many things
that we can do. And there
are some things we cannot do.
What is one thing we can't do?
Look and see.

dig

blow

build

break

sleep

awaken

walk

run

stand

sit

read

watch

draw and write

156

pull

push

kick

talk

listen

shout

whisper

eat

laugh

smile

cry

drink

jump over

crawl under

fall down

we can't fly

peek

tip a hat

go up

go down

go in

come out

WORK MACHINES

Busy, busy, busy bears. Most of the bears are busy moving dirt with their machines. But there is one bear who has a machine which does something else to the dirt. Which bear is it? What is she doing?

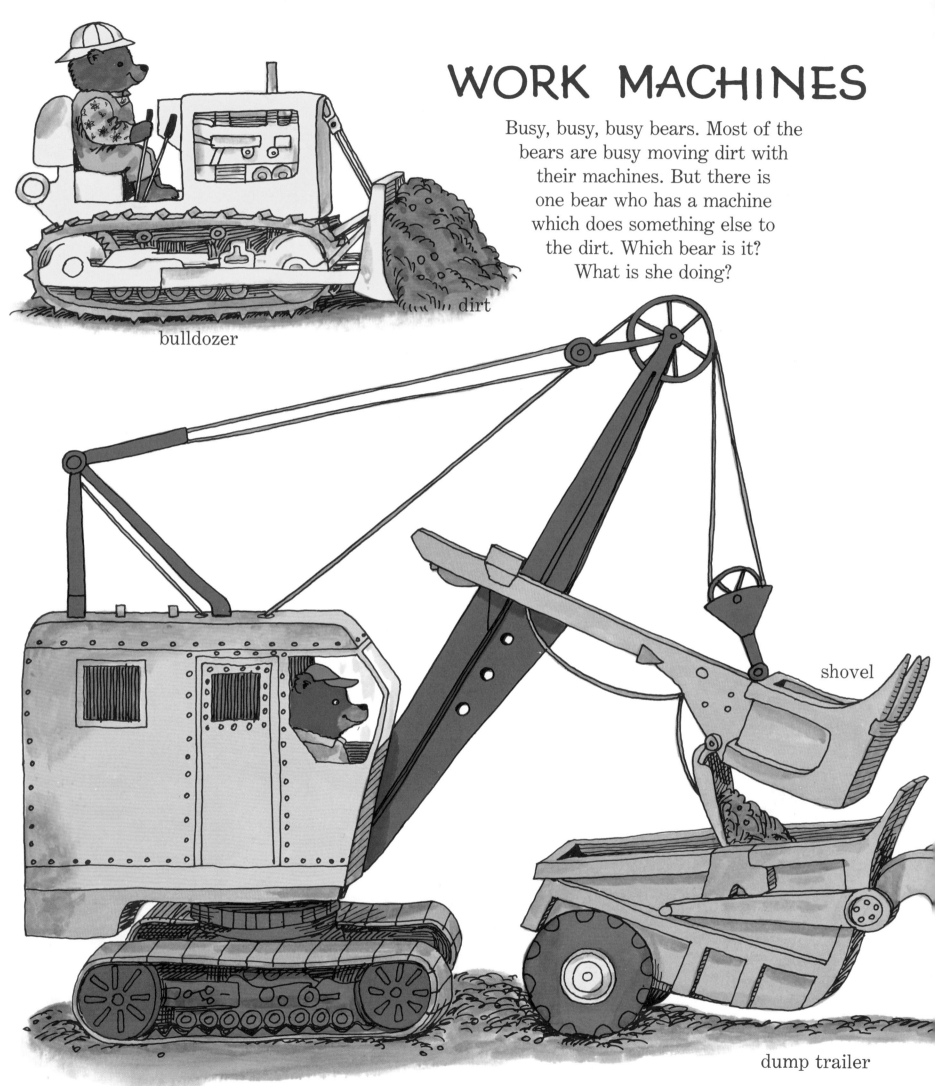

bulldozer

dirt

shovel

dump trailer

158

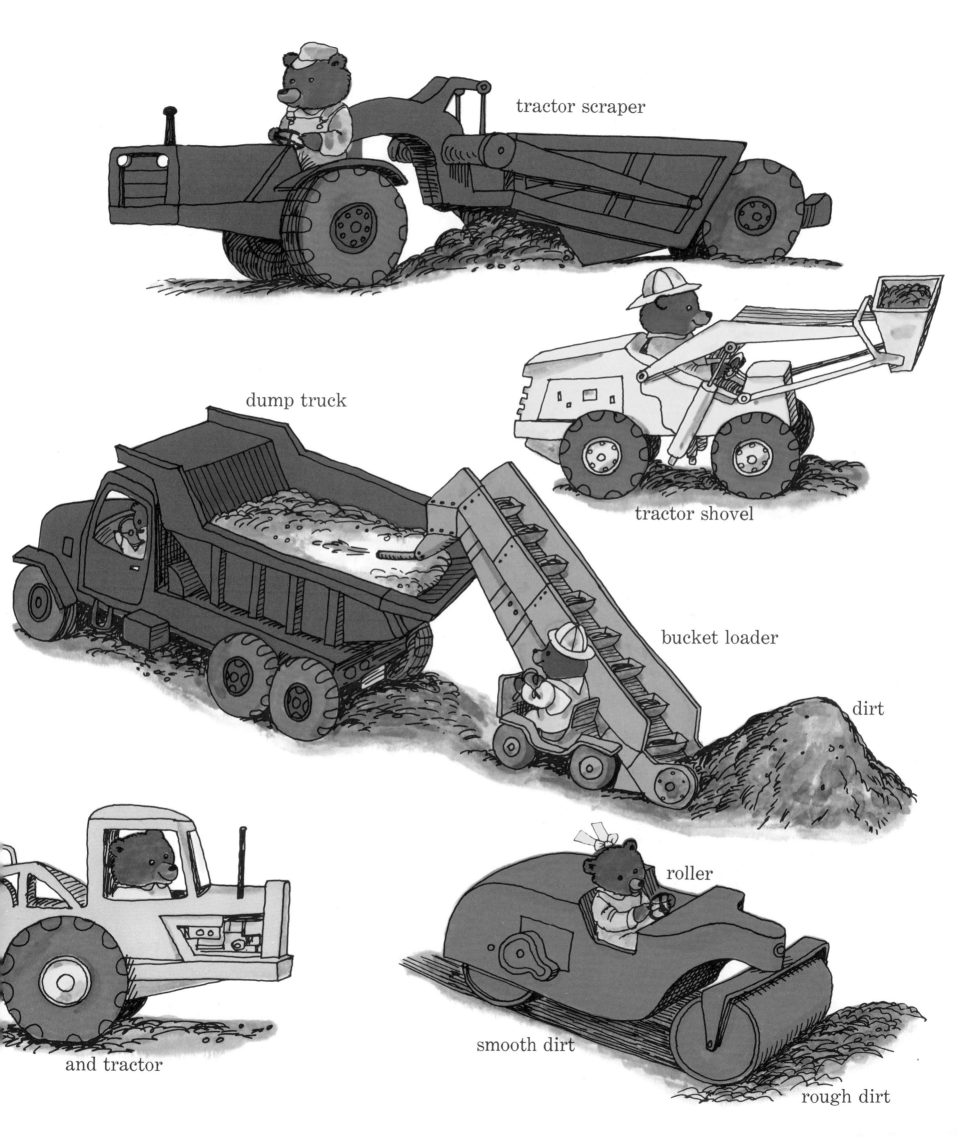

tractor scraper

tractor shovel

dump truck

bucket loader

dirt

and tractor

roller

smooth dirt

rough dirt

automobile carrier

gasoline truck

milk truck

broken-down car

tow truck

motorcycle

taxi

sports car

160

GoldenWings Freight Line

trailer truck

CARS AND TRUCKS

Down the street go the
cars and trucks.
But look! Some of the
cars don't have drivers.
Which cars have no drivers?

SANITATION
ENGINEER

garbage truck

boat trailer

station wagon

motor scooter

antique car

SCHOOL BUS

school bus

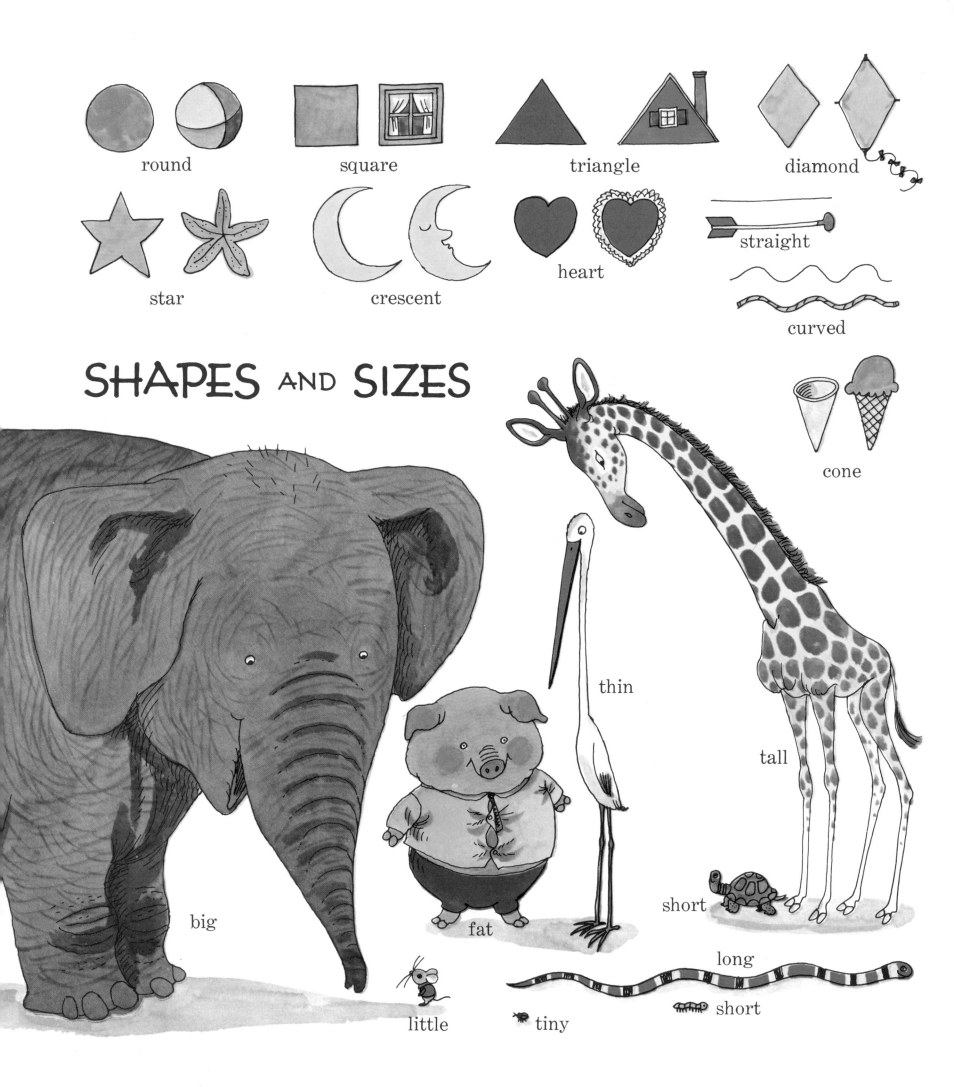

round

square

triangle

diamond

star

crescent

heart

straight

curved

cone

SHAPES AND SIZES

thin

tall

big

fat

short

long

little

tiny

short

THE BABY

father

mother

grandmother

uncle

The Cat family has a new baby kitten.
They don't know what to name it.
What would you like
to name the new baby?
Write the kitten's name here.

_ _ _ _ _ _ _ _

bottle

baby

rattle

brother

aunt

sister

diaper

grandfather

playpen

cousin

high chair

stroller

crib

bassinet

play table

walker

baby carriage

AT THE CIRCUS

The band is playing and the animals
are doing their acts. What do you like to
watch best at the circus?

tent pole

balancing pole

tightrope performer

tightrope

band

bareback rider

rope ladder

bandstand

circus horse

performing
elephant

sawdust

ring

ringmaster

trick dog

clown

pennant

circus tent

trapeze

trapeze artist

acrobat

safety net

ticket seller

hoop

lion

whip

cage

lion tamer

trained sea lion

balloon seller

popcorn seller

juggler

EDDIE

THE FIRE FIGHTERS TO THE RESCUE

Will the brave fire fighters
put out the fire in time?
I think so, don't you?

rescue truck

police car

nozzle

rear-wheel steerer

fire engine

hook-and-ladder
truck

hose

ladder

front-wheel
steerer

boots

helmet

first-aid kit

hook

bell

fire alarm box

ambulance

flames

water

smoke

fire chief

cat in danger

megaphone

fire chief's car

fire fighter

pumper

fire hydrant

ladder

F.D. 3

fire fighters

rescue net

fire fighter

fire extinguisher

bell

whistle

TRAINS

steam locomotive and tender

boxcar

Which train do you think
would be the most fun to run?
Would it be a freight train
or a passenger train?

lantern

signal tower

handcar

caboose

flatcar

railroad station

dining car

platform

conductor

baggage wagon

168

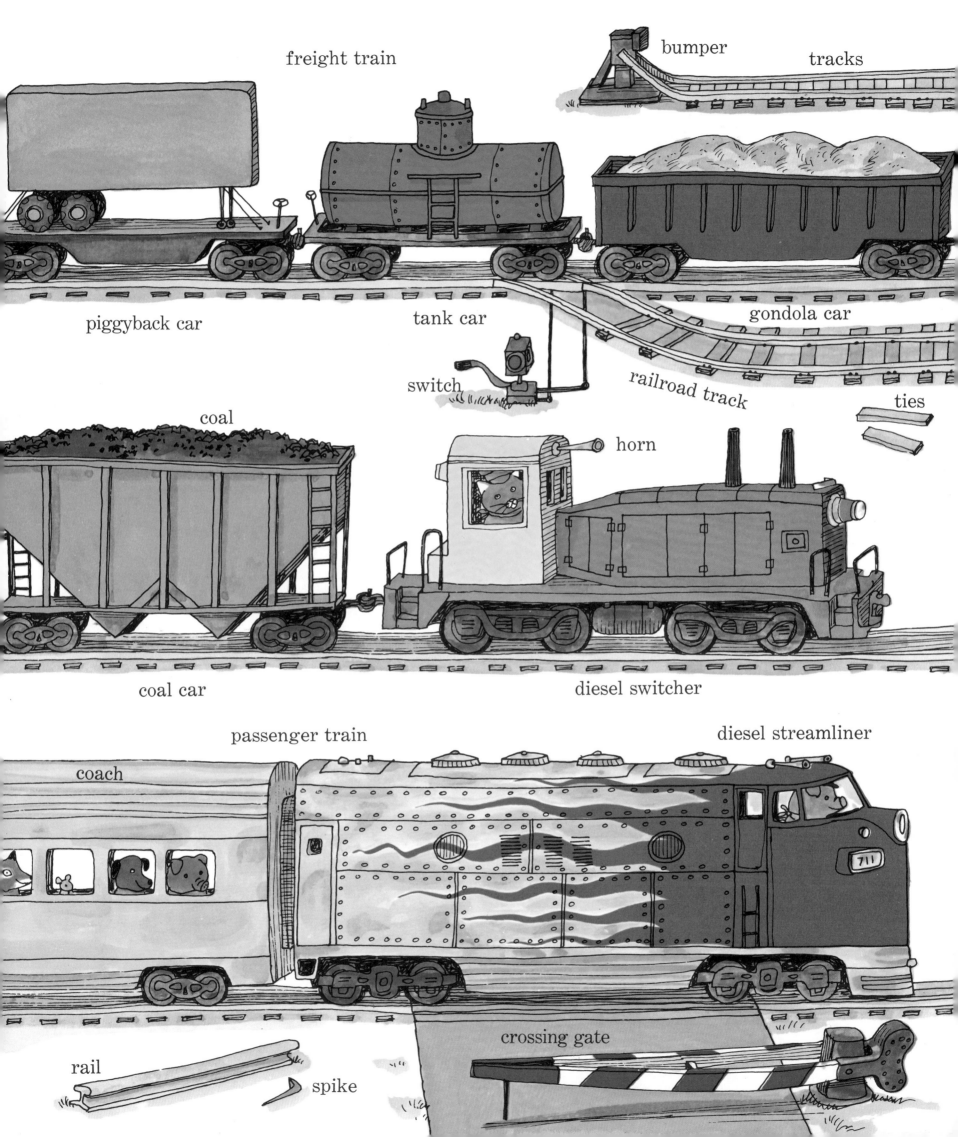

freight train

bumper

tracks

piggyback car

tank car

gondola car

switch

railroad track

ties

coal

horn

coal car

diesel switcher

passenger train

diesel streamliner

coach

711

rail

spike

crossing gate

AT THE BEACH

In the summertime it is fun
to go to the beach.
What do you think
Rabbit hears in the seashell?
Is it the sound of the waves?

telescope

lighthouse

summer cottage

oar

anchor

beach toy

shovel

rowboat

sandpiper

sand castle

waves

skate

bluefish

oyster

lobster

sea purse

scallop

hermit crab

clam

umbrella

sea gull

sun

pavilion

lifeguard

flagpole

sand dune

boardwalk

beach grass

stairs

bathhouse

beach chair

seashell

sand fort

starfish

waves

shrimp

minnow

horseshoe crab

crab

seaweed

flounder

mussel

171

MAKING THINGS GROW

Everyone is working in the garden.
Mr. Crow has a seed in his mouth.
Do you think he will plant it?
Or will he eat it?

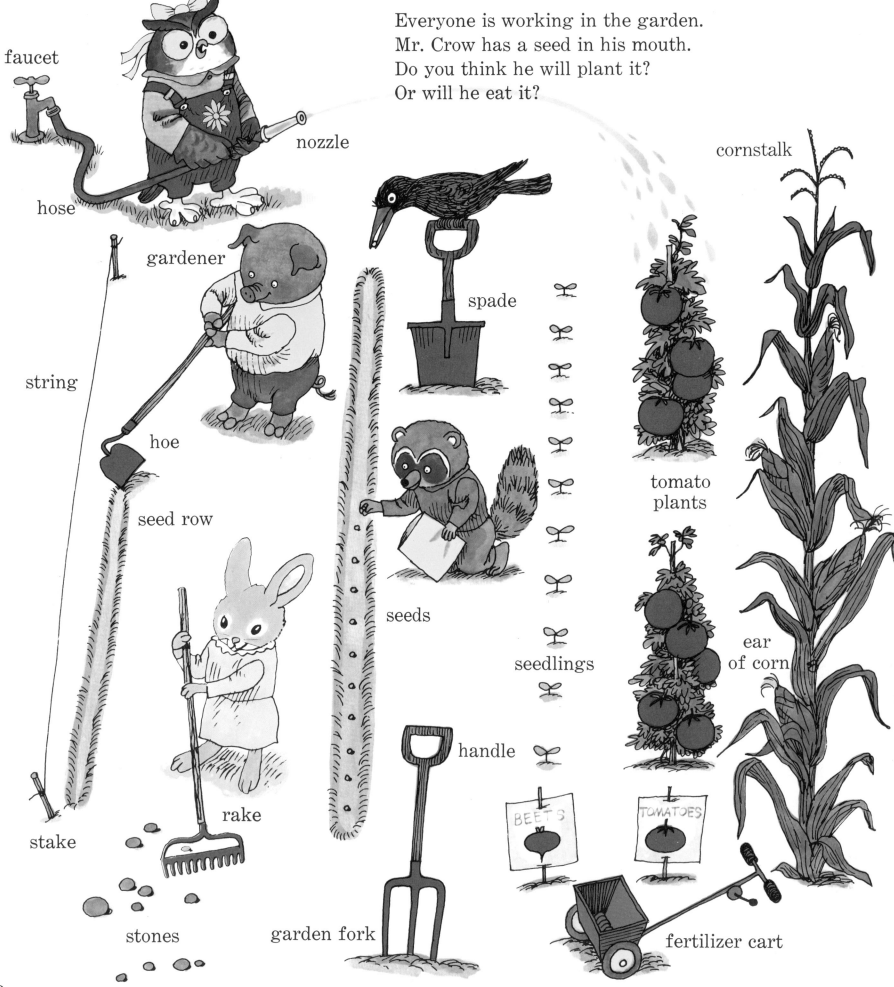

faucet

nozzle

hose

gardener

string

hoe

seed row

stake

rake

stones

garden fork

handle

spade

seeds

seedlings

BEETS

TOMATOES

cornstalk

tomato
plants

ear
of corn

fertilizer cart

THE WEATHER

sun

cloud

When we go outdoors we see what the weather is like. Sometimes it is sunny. Sometimes it is cloudy. It can be windy, or cold, or hot. It can be snowing or raining. What was the weather like outdoors today? What is your favorite kind of weather?

lightning

rain

hailstones

snowflakes

thermometer

rainbow

windmill

wind

hat

foxtail grass

raindrops

toad

toadstool

ladybug

a cat chasing a hat

puddle

mud

kite

rain shower

plow

robin

buds

nest

SPRING

Look at that baby lamb hop!
It is spring. She is happy.
Look at Mr. Bear coming out of
his cave! It is spring. He is happy.
Now he can use his new
lawn mower.

tree

lamb

bush

bridge

brook

cave

fern

turtle

roots

spring peeper

pussy willow

daffodil

lawn mower

crocus

violets

174

SUMMER

cow

meadow

calf

cornfield

fence

Do you like to go
on picnics in the summertime?
Ants just love to go to picnics.
Do you know why?

station wagon

tent

fly

screen

cooking grill

charcoal

picnic basket

cooler

hamburger

charcoal bag

ketchup

hotdog

mustard

pickle

mosquito

pole

paper cup

rock

ants

bobber

cattails

frog

dock

pond

water lily

dragonfly

pebbles

stones

175

sun

duck

falling leaves

gate

stone wall

corn shock

nuts

pumpkin

roadside stand

Indian corn

cider

jelly

squash

basket of apples

FALL

In the fall the air gets colder. The green leaves turn to bright colors. Then they fall to the ground. Is that why we say it is fall at this time of year? Maybe it is.

smoke

flames

turkey

rake

bonfire

leaves

176

snowstorm

WINTER

There are many ways to have fun on the snow and ice. Maybe you would like to do all of them. Would you?

sleigh

icicle

fishing shack

skis

sled

toboggan

ice fishing

snow

ice-skating rink

ice skater

snowball

hockey stick

puck

ice skates

muffler

spare tire

jeep

snowplow

a pig all wrapped up

snowman

LITTLE THINGS

Here are many little things.
What little thing do you sometimes
put on your bedroom wall?

worm

dandelion seed

button

spool

thread

fly

ant

drop of water

ladybug

bead

snowflake

pin

fingerprint

petal

mosquito

butterfly

fishhook

crumb

bubble

peanut

tack

pen point

tea leaf

gumdrop

pea

caterpillar

jelly bean

firefly

ring

sand

blueberry

moth

rice

polliwog

keyhole

shell

marble

blade of grass

paper clip

cricket

raisin

beetle

raspberry

thimble

pincushion

hermit crab

pebble

sea horse

bee

mushroom

pearl

ink spot

confetti

feather

splinter

bean

safety pin

baby mouse

dot

PARTS OF THE BODY

Bears use their paws to pick things up.
What do you use?

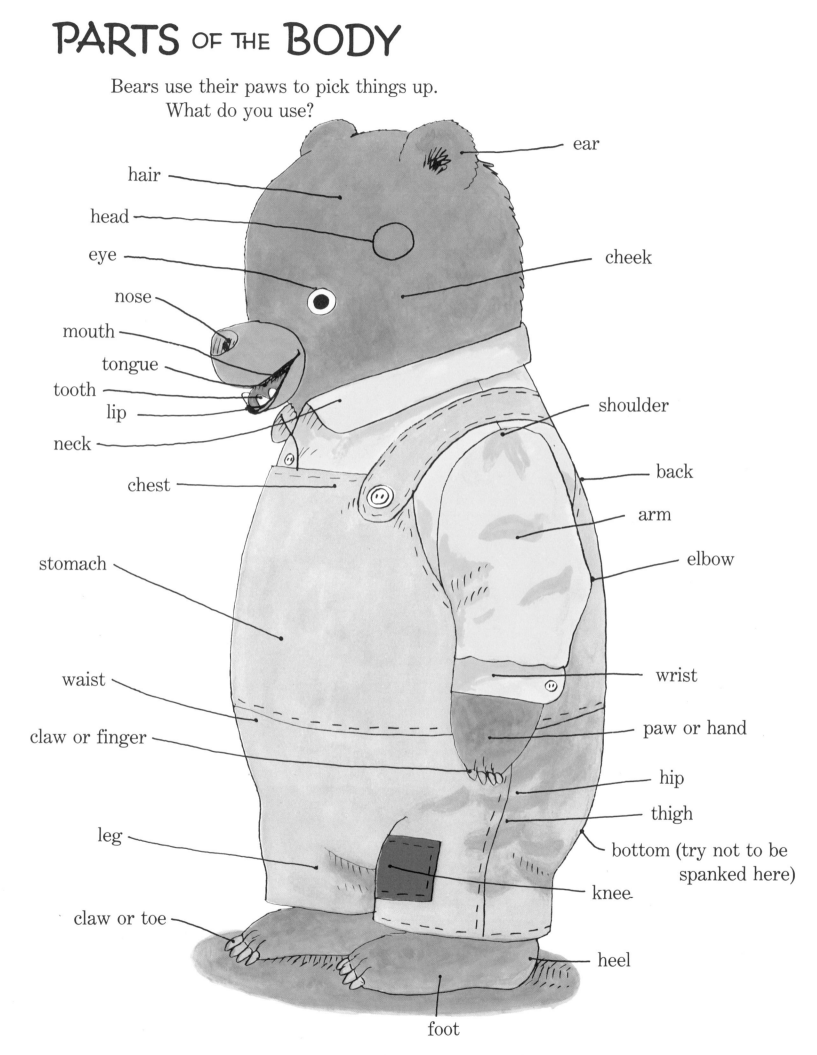

ear

hair

head

eye

cheek

nose

mouth

tongue

tooth

lip

neck

shoulder

back

arm

elbow

chest

stomach

waist

wrist

claw or finger

paw or hand

hip

thigh

leg

bottom (try not to be
spanked here)

knee

claw or toe

heel

foot

BEDTIME

Little Elephant is getting ready for bed.
But who is that hiding under the bed?
Find that rascal and tell her to brush her
teeth and get ready for bed, too.

shower

faucet

medicine
cabinet

brush

shower
curtain

toothpaste

soapsuds

sink

bathtub

towel

bath mat

slippers

toilet

bathroom

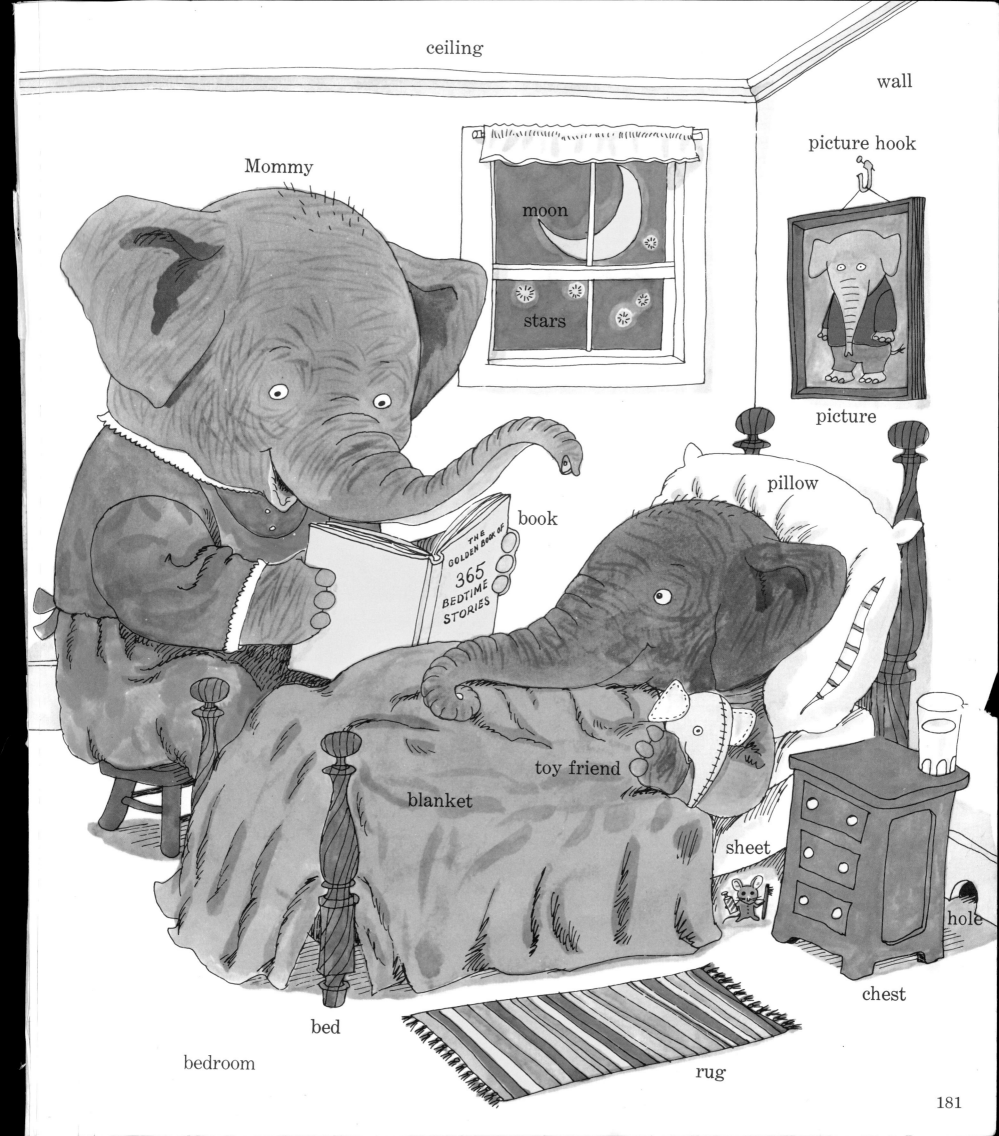

ceiling

wall

Mommy

picture hook

moon

stars

picture

pillow

book

toy friend

blanket

sheet

hole

chest

bed

bedroom

rug

181

NUMBERS

How high can you count?
Can you count up to
twenty ladybugs?
I'll bet you can.

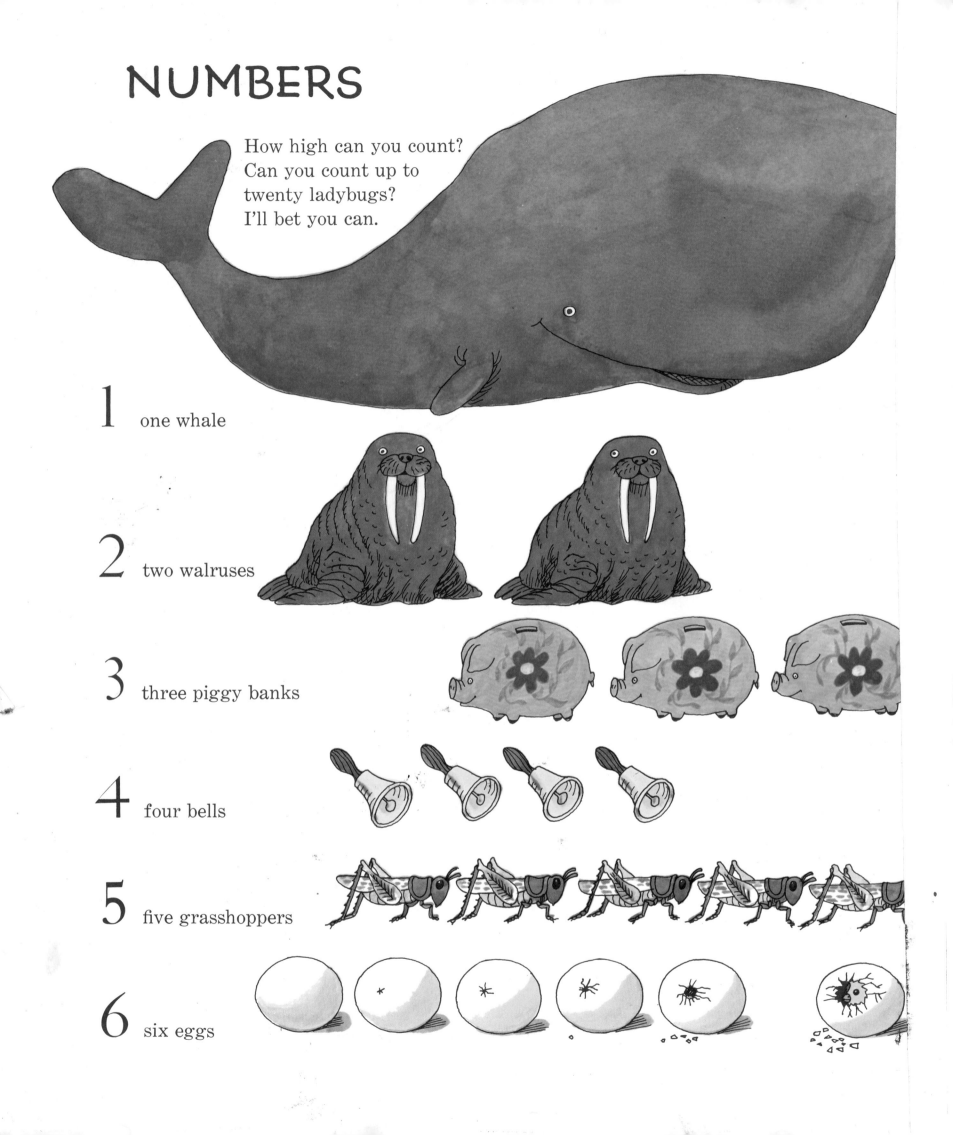

1 one whale

2 two walruses

3 three piggy banks

4 four bells

5 five grasshoppers

6 six eggs